MUCH IN EVIDENCE

HENRY CECIL

*

Much in Evidence

London
MICHAEL JOSEPH

First published by
MICHAEL JOSEPH LTD
26 *Bloomsbury Street,*
*London, W.C.*1
1957

Set and printed in Great Britain by Tonbridge Printers Ltd,
Peach Hall Works, Tonbridge, Kent, in Baskerville ten
on twelve point, on paper made by Henry Bruce at Currie,
Midlothian, and bound by James Burn at Esher, Surrey

CONTENTS

CHAPTER ONE

Breaking and Entering

WILLIAM RICHMOND lay in bed reading a detective novel. Outside two men were making preparations for breaking into his house. Mr Richmond was an ardent but critical reader of crime stories. By the side of his bed were several he had discarded after reading a few chapters.

'Perfectly absurd. He'd have gone to the police at once,' he had said aloud. 'It's too ridiculous the way innocent people build up a case against themselves in books and plays. They'd never do it in real life. Tripe.' He had tried another for rather longer. Then he had put that down too.

'Why on earth should he tell those lies? Just to help the author with his plot. Can't think of any other reason.'

But while the two men outside were considering the best method of making an entry he had found another book which pleased him more.

'Alibis,' began the first chapter, 'should be acted in advance before you commit your crime. Go through all the motions with your confederates and don't say a word or do a thing which would not be said or done if the meeting were a genuine one. Then, later on, if you have to give evidence about it, you only have to lie about the date or time. What you say took place at the meeting will really have taken place. It is so much easier to give convincing evidence of things which have really happened.'

'How right you are,' said Mr Richmond. 'You should have been one yourself. But p'raps you are.'

He looked at the author's name.

It was Simon Spinette.

'Obviously a pseudonym,' commented Mr Richmond. 'I wonder who he is. Oh, well—what does it matter—so long as he sends me to sleep.'

He went on reading for some time, while the men outside the house continued their operations with the greatest caution. They discarded about as many windows as Mr Richmond discarded detective works. Too difficult or too noisy. It was not going to be a particularly easy job.

'Well,' said Mr Richmond eventually, 'time for sleep. Thank you, Mr Spinette. You haven't put a foot wrong so far. Finish you tomorrow. Good night.'

He switched off the light and turned on his left side. After a few minutes he turned on his right. Then back again. Not long afterwards he swore and switched on the light again. He leaned out of bed and put on the wireless. He was rewarded by gentle dance music. He had just started to feel the first beautiful moments of oncoming sleep when the music stopped abruptly and instead a voice said:

'Can't you sleep? Dear, dear. Let me see if I can help you. Turn on your right side.'

'I won't,' murmured Mr Richmond.

'Come on now,' went on the voice persuasively, 'it's for your own good you know. Now take three deep breaths.'

'Rubbish,' said Mr Richmond in the vernacular.

'One—two—three—that's right,' said the voice. 'We'll soon have you sleeping like a baby.'

Mr Richmond repeated his observation. There was a pause as though the broadcaster might have taken offence. If it was so, he soon recovered.

'Asleep yet?' he asked. 'No? Dear, dear, dear. Something more is required. I'm afraid you must get up.'

'I'll do nothing of the sort,' said Mr Richmond.

'Go to your medicine cabinet,' continued the voice, 'and take out your bottle of Sleepybye tablets. Take two tablets—

what? You haven't got any? That's terrible. Make a note of the name and get them first thing in the morning—that's if you want a really lovely, cosy, restful night tomorrow. Absolutely harmless and no doctor's prescription needed—but, don't forget, they must be Sleepybye. Sleepybye. That's it. Try saying it to yourself. Sleepybye, Sleepybye, Sleepybye. The very name should help you. Good night. Sleep well—and, if you don't, remember to buy some in the morning—every chemist should have them. What's the name? Come along— what is it?'

'Sleepybye,' said Mr Richmond rather unwillingly.

'That's right—Sleepybye it is. Good for you. Very good for you indeed. Now how about some more dance music, which comes to you through the courtesy of the Sleepybye Company Ltd., makers of the only genuine Sleepybye tablets.'

Meanwhile the men outside had met with some success and had managed to open a window. They climbed through, and very cautiously started to make their way through the house, listening intently for any sign which might suggest that someone was about. Having satisfied themselves that all was quiet, they sat down for a moment and one of them opened a large bag. From it he took out two false noses and two Father Christmas beards. They put them on and then began as cautiously as before to search the house. But on their way they unbolted the front door and left it on the latch, presumably to enable them to make a quick getaway. After some time, while Mr Richmond was dozing gently to the accompaniment of the music so considerately supplied by the Sleepybye Company, they discovered the safe. They gave it a short examination, during which neither spoke a word. Then one of them shook his head and pointed to the keyhole. The other pointed to the ceiling. His companion nodded. Then together they started, quietly and with the same care which they had shown throughout, to go up the stairs. Half-way up they stopped and listened. For the first time they heard the sound of the Sleepy-bye music, which Mr Richmond had kept on very softly. They turned to each other and waited on the stairs. One of them produced a spanner. The other nodded. They adjusted their noses and beards and continued quietly up the stairs until they reached Mr Richmond's bedroom door. The man who was not holding the spanner raised his hand. As soon as his companion nodded he opened the door and they burst into the room.

'What the——!' began Mr Richmond and switched on the light.

'Don't make a sound or move,' said the first Father Christmas, 'or you'll get a dose of this,' and he showed Mr Richmond the spanner. 'I mean it,' he added menacingly.

'What d'you want?' asked Mr Richmond.

'Keys,' said the second Father.

Mr Richmond looked at the men—who appeared a strange mixture of menace and benevolence.

'Collecting for Christmas?' he asked eventually, with a not very convincing smile.

'You won't see another if you don't hand over those keys—and quick. Now, don't move—tell us where they are.'

After a little hesitation, during which the Father with the spanner took a step towards him, Mr Richmond pointed to a drawer. The other Father went to the drawer and took out some keys. Without another word he went out of the room, but before he did so he just pointed towards Mr Richmond, clearly indicating that his collaborator was to look after their host while he attended to the safe. When he had left, Mr Richmond eventually said:

'D'you think you'll get away with this?'

'Shut up.'

After about a quarter of an hour the other man reappeared with their bag. He nodded to his confederate. He then took out some cord from his pocket, with which they proceeded to tie up Mr Richmond.

'You'll be sorry for this,' said Richmond.

'Not as sorry as you,' said the man with the spanner—and struck him smartly on the head.

Mr Richmond groaned slightly and a few minutes later the men left him. The dance music was still being played. Suddenly it was interrupted by the original broadcaster: 'Asleep yet?' he asked.

CHAPTER TWO

The Claim

IT was not for some little time that Mr Richmond was able to free himself. He dialled 999. He seemed to find it quite an effort; 111 would have been much easier.

'What number are you speaking from?' he was asked.

'Oh, God,' he said, and dropped the receiver.

'Hullo—hullo,' he heard the operator saying.

He picked up the receiver again.

'Burglars—knock on head—7 Pendlebury Gardens,' he said.

'You want the police,' said the operator.

Mr Richmond smiled faintly.

'No, the florists,' he said.

Within a very few minutes a police car was on its way to 7 Pendlebury Gardens. Obtaining no answer the police broke in through the door, only to find they had come to the wrong Pendlebury Gardens. Eventually they came to the right house. They had to break in there too, as Mr Richmond did not feel well enough to go downstairs and let them in. His knock on the head was not very severe but they sent for his doctor, who bandaged his head and gave him a sedative. Then they took a statement from him. He described the men as well as he could but, in view of the noses and beards, there was not much for the police to go on. Had they taken anything? Well, he hadn't looked yet, but they'd taken the keys to his safe—where he had placed £100,000 in notes the night before.

'They must have learned of it,' he told the police officers. 'I only put it there last night. If you ask me, they've a confederate in the bank—a messenger or someone, I expect.'

They went at once to search the safe, but, as they suspected, the money was gone.

'One hundred thousand pounds! That's a lot of money,' said the Detective Sergeant. 'I hope you're insured.'

'Fortunately,' said Mr Richmond. 'But I very nearly didn't bother. It was only for one night, you know. But the bank manager persuaded me. I'm damned grateful. Don't grudge the premium any more.'

Shortly after he had made his claim Mr Richmond was visited by a representative of a firm of claims assessors—Waite & Harvitt, who were employed by his insurers, the Positive Insurance Company Ltd. He was surprised to find it was a woman, a Miss Rosamund Clinch. She was small and attractive, aged about thirty-five, with a normally mild and unassuming manner which concealed an armoury of high explosive.

'I do hope,' she said, 'that you feel well enough to discuss your claim, Mr Richmond.'

'Quite, thank you. I was lucky really. It was only a glancing blow; the blood made it seem worse than it was.'

'I hate blood,' said Miss Clinch.

'Cigarette?' said Mr Richmond.

'Thank you, no,' said Miss Clinch. 'Now I'm afraid I must ask you a lot of questions. If you feel tired, please tell me and I'll come back another day.'

'You're most considerate.'

'Not at all. I'm sure you'll understand that the Company is naturally a little concerned about the claim. A hundred thousand pounds is a lot of money. They don't normally insure cash, and for a loss to occur within twelve hours or so of the insurance being placed is a little disturbing.'

'Fire ahead,' said Mr Richmond. 'Ask anything you like. I shan't tell you any more lies than I can help.'

'Perhaps it's only fair to warn you,' said Miss Clinch, 'that if you tell me *any* lies it entitles the Company to repudiate the claim altogether.'

'It was a joke, Miss Clinch.'

'I'm afraid,' replied Miss Clinch, 'that the Company doesn't consider the loss of a hundred thousand pounds to be a joke.'

'I'm so sorry. I'll be serious.'

'Thank you,' said Miss Clinch. 'That will be most helpful.'

'Think nothing of it,' said Mr Richmond. 'That was just a manner of speaking,' he added hastily. 'Naturally you will think a lot about it.'

'Mr Richmond,' said Miss Clinch, 'the Company doesn't care for facetiousness in a claim form, and I am recording every word you say.'

Mr Richmond looked surprised.

'But you're not writing,' he said.

'On the tablets of my mind, Mr Richmond. If I want to, I can retain in my memory entire conversations of half an hour or more until I can get to a typewriter and transcribe them.'

'Do you use shorthand?' queried Mr Richmond. 'But no, I suppose you wouldn't.'

'As a matter of fact, I do.'

'So anything I say is recorded in your mind as pot-hooks and squiggles and things. How interesting. I wonder if they'd show up in an X-ray?'

'If minds showed up in an X-ray, Mr Richmond, the Company would like to see what is in your mind at the moment. It would save a lot of trouble. But perhaps you'll forgive me if we get down to business. Why did you draw out a hundred thousand pounds all at one time, may I ask?'

'To use on racecourses.'

'Rather a lot, was it not?'

'I wanted to win a lot.'

'Have you ever done such a thing before?'

'Not to the same extent. But I've never had a hundred thousand pounds before. Represents the savings of a lifetime.'

'Saved out of what, Mr Richmond?'

'Winnings, Miss Clinch. As you should know, I'm a professional punter. I've made a lot of money and I wanted to make a lot more.'

'Who knew you were taking such a large sum to your home?'

'My bank manager—and anybody he told, I suppose. The cashier who brought in the money—I was given it in the manager's office, in case there were any prying eyes about.'

'Have you ever had a similar burglary?'

'Never had one at all, as far as I can remember. I believe my parents once had one, but I was too young to remember properly. I have a vague idea of something happening.'

'What was stolen then?'

'I've no idea. Jewellery, I expect—but I don't really know. There wasn't much to be stolen in those days.'

'Have you made any claims at all on insurance companies?'

'Certainly not.'

'None at all?'

'No.'

'I take it then that no company has ever refused to insure you?'

'None.'

'Well, thank you, Mr Richmond,' said Miss Clinch. 'I'll go and have this typed out and then perhaps you wouldn't mind signing it.'

'With pleasure. When will the claim be paid? I want the money badly. It's holding me up.'

'As soon as the Company is satisfied,' said Miss Clinch, 'but you can't expect it to hand out a hundred thousand pounds as though it were a currant bun.'

'I gave them my premium without any fuss. I've answered all your questions, and I expect to be paid. It's bad luck, I know, but that's one of the risks your people run. They should insure against it.'

'There will be no undue delay, Mr Richmond.'

'I'm sorry to be blunt,' said Mr Richmond, 'but there will be no delay at all. If I'm not paid I'll sue. I'm not going to be played about with.'

'You can be as blunt as you jolly well please,' said Miss Clinch. 'You'll be paid when the Company is satisfied, and not before. Good afternoon.'

CHAPTER THREE

The Claim Considered

A week after her interview with Mr Richmond, Miss Clinch discussed his claim with Mr Waite, the senior partner in Waite and Harvitt.

'This claim stinks,' she said.

'I dare say it does,' said Mr Waite, 'but you can't plead that as a defence to it. What we want are facts, not feminine intuition. Let me hasten to add, though, that your intuition is nearly always right.'

'Nearly always? When has it not been, may I ask?'

'I beg your pardon. Always right.'

'It follows from that,' said Miss Clinch, 'that it is in all probability right this time. Any statistician would tell you that.'

'I don't require a statistician. Why do you think we pay you such a large salary? As far as I know, you're the only woman assessor and you're worth much more than your inconsiderable weight in hard cash to us and our clients.'

'Very good of you to say so,' said Miss Clinch, 'but though I like my salary and venture to think that I earn it, it isn't the money which interests me—it's the intense satisfaction which the work gives me. I love arriving at the truth. Which leads me back to Mr Richmond. I'm damned if I'm going to let underwriters pay this claim. It's a fraud if ever there was one.'

'Miss Clinch,' said Mr Waite, 'no one could say that I have ever encouraged the payment of claims. I think I may say with some justification that I have worn down more claimants than most assessors. Indeed I invented a form of correspondence which has now become almost standard in many offices. It takes a very hardened and knowledgeable claimant to withstand my delaying tactics. By the time I've finished with them they're glad to take half the claim. Once they go to a solicitor they've got the law costs piling up against them. Oh, no, Miss Clinch, you don't have to convince me on the subject of not paying claims. I'm not a convert—I'm an addict—a high priest you might say.'

'Mr Waite,' said Miss Clinch, 'it is not my business to criticize my superiors, though I confess that one of the things I like about this office is the latitude I am given in this respect. May I say, however, that I entirely disagree with your methods of business? Honest claims should be paid in full and as quickly as possible. If it were my job in this office to wear down decent policy holders, who have paid premiums for years and have never made a claim before, I should have resigned long ago. Your tactics are in my humble opinion almost as dishonest as those of the people who make fraudulent claims. When you arrange for underwriters to pay half the value of an honest claim you're allowing them to stick to the other half without the slightest justification. If that isn't fraud I don't know what is. I know the law doesn't call it so, but I do. If you owe a man a shilling and keep him waiting so long for it and write so many letters about it that he's glad to take sixpence in the end, it's as bad as pinching something out of a shop. However, there it is. It's not easy for a woman to get a job of this sort, and I can't pick and choose. But what I like is hunting for the truth. I'm a detective by instinct and this job is meat and drink to me. I don't wear any of your claimants down. I find out if the claim's a genuine one. It's thrilling, Mr Waite. I don't care whether a claim's false or true. I like arriving at the truth with as near to certainty as you can have in human affairs.'

'Well, Miss Clinch,' said Mr Waite, 'now that you've got that off your chest, what's your near certainty in this case?'

'I feel it in my bones,' said Miss Clinch.

'Let me see,' mused Mr Waite, 'how would that look as a defence? The Defendants feel it in their bones that the claim is fraudulent.'

'Flippancy costs nothing—but it gets us nowhere,' said Miss Clinch.

'All right,' said Mr Waite, 'let's get down to facts. What are they? There's no doubt his house was broken into, is there? The police have found the marks, and he undoubtedly had a bang on the head.'

'He may have done it all himself,' said Miss Clinch. 'Anyone could fake a breaking in. And it wasn't a hard blow he gave himself anyway.'

'So you've decided that already, have you? But how can you prove it?'

'It's for him to prove it happened, not for us to prove it didn't.'

'All right. Lets continue with the facts. There's no doubt he took a hundred thousand pounds out of the bank, is there?'

'No—that's true enough—but I'd like to know where it is.'

'You saw the bank manager yourself, and he confirms that it was on his suggestion that the money was insured.'

'That's true in a way,' said Miss Clinch. 'But suppose I'm right and the man is a crook; it would be pretty simple to get a bank manager to advise you that—wouldn't it? I agree with you that it's a useful bit of evidence for Richmond that his bank manager will say that it was he who advised the insurance. But put yourself in Richmond's position. You wouldn't have to be so brilliant to realize that in advance, would you, and, if you realize it, all you have to do is to wait till the manager says—as he's almost bound to do—"I suppose it's insured for the night?" Then you express a natural reluctance to pay the premium and grudgingly allow yourself to be overruled by the expert: "Well, Mr Manager—if you say so—I suppose I'd better. D'you know anyone who'd do it for me?" If the worst comes to the worst, and the manager doesn't come up to scratch and ask if it's insured, you can always raise the matter yourself. "It isn't worth insuring just for the night, I suppose? I never have in the past." It's all too simple.'

'That's on the assumption that the man is a crook. But what are the rest of the facts? He *was* going to a race meeting up North and he *did* have to catch a train before the banks opened. He *has* been to race meetings. Tote Investors *have* paid him a lot of money.'

'I dare say,' said Miss Clinch, 'but, if I have my way, our people are not going to. This is a fraudulent claim if ever there was one. False noses and Father Christmas beards! It stinks, Mr Waite, it stinks.'

While Mr Waite and Miss Clinch were considering the claim from their point of view, Mr Richmond was on the way to his solicitors, Messrs Bogg, Tewkesbury and Company, to discuss the same subject from his point of view. Mr Tewkesbury, who was the sole proprietor of the firm, had been a solicitor for many years. He had had a classical education and was not without ability, but unfortunately his mind and body had for so long and so consistently been soaked with whisky that, even when he was sober—which was seldom—he was so muddle-headed and so unaware of it that it was difficult to extract much sense out of him. Occasionally he had flashes of brilliance, but they only served to emphasize the dark clouds in which his mind usually resided. His business had naturally very much deteriorated and, indeed, to those who are unaware of the extent to which the public obstinately persists in consulting professional men of proved stupidity it must have been almost incredible that he had a practice at all.

Before Mr Richmond arrived at his office Mr Tewkesbury had been interviewing a client about an accident case. He was comparatively sober at the beginning of the interview, but, before long, he had managed to improve on that position by arranging with his sole employee, a Miss Winter, to summon him to the outer office from time to time where he was able to take several most pleasurable pulls at a flask. By the time his client had left him he had reached the desired stage of intoxication and was ready to proceed with the rest of the day's work. It was at this moment that Mr Richmond was shown into his room.

'Come in, my dear sir, come in,' said Mr Tewkesbury. 'And what can our firm have the pleasure of doing for Mr Richmond?'

'Just a letter, I'm afraid. That's all. Don't suppose it will come to anything more.'

Mr Tewkesbury tried to conceal his disappointment. Even a long letter could not be converted into more than a glass or two. Still, even a glass or two was a pleasant thought. He brightened at the prospect.

'A letter, sir, a letter. It shall be done. Miss Winter, bring in your note-book, please.'

A plain girl, who sniffed, came in. There had been a time when Mr Tewkesbury combined whisky with other pleasures, but now whisky was in sole and absolute command. In consequence the standard of beauty among the stenographers employed by Bogg, Tewkesbury & Co. had sunk dismally. The plain girl spoke loudly and clearly.

'Did you send for me, sir?' she asked, in a dull, uninterested, unintelligent Cockney voice.

'I did. Take a letter, please. Dear Sir, we have been consulted by our client, Mr . . . I'm so sorry, I've forgotten your name, sir . . . of course—of course—I'm so sorry, unforgivable— Mr William Richmond—in regard to a bottle of whisky—I beg your pardon, sir, just for the moment I'm confusing your case . . . your case . . .'

He trailed off. For the moment the only thing with which he could associate the word 'case'—it was a beautiful thought —was a case of whisky. But one letter wouldn't run to a bottle, let alone a case.

'I haven't yet told you what I've come about, Mr Tewkesbury,' said Mr Richmond.

'Then why,' said Mr Tewkesbury, 'then why should I have sent for Miss Winter, sir?'

'I've no idea,' said Mr Richmond.

'Remarkable,' said Mr Tewkesbury. 'Very well, then, that will be all for the moment, Miss Winter. Just a top and one carbon, please.'

Miss Winter left the room.

'Now, sir,' said Mr Tewkesbury. 'You were telling me about your case. Where was the accident?'

'It wasn't exactly an accident,' said Mr Richmond.

'Call it what you will, sir. The collision if you prefer it. Both cars were stationary at the time no doubt, but they managed to collide all right fortunately. What would we do, sir, if they didn't? If it weren't for tobacco and accidents where would the country be? Now tell me, sir, were you badly injured? Shock, of course, we know—but actual injuries; it's to be hoped there were some abrasions at least, if no actual bones broken. I prefer a broken bone or two if possible, though I'm bound to say, sir, that they're cheap enough nowadays. Judges aren't what they were, sir. I'd like to have a few of *their* legs off, sir. That might change their tune a bit. Might take a few of their heads off too, sir, while I was about it. But tell me, sir, where did you say you were hurt?'

'Well—it was my head, as a matter of fact.'

'The head, sir. Capital. Capital. Forgive my classicism, sir. But seriously, sir, we can make a lot out of that. No one can say what the result of a head injury may be. You've headaches of course, sir, and you've lost your memory too perhaps, and I'll guarantee, sir, that you get irritable now when you used to be as quiet and peaceful as a salmon on a slab—a dead one of course, sir, though I'm not a fisherman myself. And then I don't expect you can read any more, sir, and no theatres or cinemas for you—while music sends you screaming out of the room, sir; that's right, isn't it, sir, screaming out of the room? And think of it, sir,' said Mr Tewkesbury sadly, 'you used to play the violin with your old mother. It's a shame, sir, these motorists think they own the road. Miss Winter, please.'

Miss Winter came in and sat down.

'Did you send for me, sir?' she said.

'Take a letter, please,' said Mr Tewkesbury briskly. 'As I was saying, sir, these motorists—no concern for anyone except themselves—speed, sir, speed. That's all it is. From A to B as fast as possible. Then from B to C even faster. Finally from C to A faster still. A, B and C are not places, sir. They are pedestrians.'

A sudden thought struck Mr Tewkesbury.

'You weren't driving yourself I suppose, sir?' he asked.

'No,' said Mr Richmond, 'I was in bed.'

'In bed, sir, in bed? That'll add to the damages. Not satisfied with catching you in the road, have to chase you into your own house. It's a scandal, that's what it is, sir, a scandal. I'll make them pay in this case, you leave it to me, sir. Thank you, Miss Winter. Now don't dawdle, girl, off with you—I want that letter at once. Mr Richmond's a busy man. So am I. What are you waiting for? Come, come, if you're going to stay in this office you'll have to step it more lively than that. Off with you.'

Miss Winter left the room. Mr Tewkesbury sighed.

'Staff problems, sir? You don't have to talk to me about staff problems. That girl's both in one. She's the staff and the problem. Wonder how long she'll take over that letter? Bet she's got it down wrong. But I'll correct it, sir. Don't you worry, sir. It's all here.'

Mr Tewkesbury tapped his head.

'Once I've dictated a letter I never forget it, sir—never. This is full of dictated letters, sir. I could reel them out to you, sir, one after the other and not a comma misplaced. A wonderful thing the brain, sir—which reminds me, your head. You had concussion, of course, sir. Any giddiness, sir? Stand up and turn round six times quickly. We'll soon see. And what about taste, sir? I'll warrant you don't enjoy your food, sir, as you

used to? And I expect you had a pretty palate for a glass of
wine, sir—which reminds me, sir—just about this time in the
morning I usually go . . . I don't know if you'd care to accom-
pany me, sir? She'll have the letter ready when we get
back.'

CHAPTER FOUR

Silence in Court

IN spite of Mr Tewkesbury's staff and alcoholic problems, a letter was actually received by Messrs Waite & Harvitt, from Messrs Bogg, Tewkesbury & Co., stating that, unless Mr Richmond's claim was met forthwith, a writ would be issued.

'I must have more time,' said Miss Clinch. 'He'll have to sue.'

'I don't like it,' said Mr Waite, 'but if we let them go ahead will you guarantee something before we get into Court?'

'I'll guarantee nothing,' said Miss Clinch, 'except that Mr Richmond didn't lose a hundred thousand pounds or any part thereof—as they say.'

'Who's going to pay the costs if we lose?'

'Now really!' said Miss Clinch. 'The costs are a flea-bite compared with a hundred thousand pounds. This isn't like a claim for eightpence halfpenny. It's worth a bit extra to have a chance of getting the evidence. I must have more time. Once you pay him, you've had it. You'd never get it back.'

'All right,' said Mr Waite. 'I'll put it up to the company and see what the directors say.'

In consequence of what they said, a writ was duly issued on behalf of Mr Richmond, and the battle began. Just before the time arrived when a defence had to be delivered on behalf of the Company, Mr Waite sent for Miss Clinch.

'Well,' he said, 'got any forrader?'

'Not really,' said Miss Clinch, 'though we have got a defence of a sort—not the kind I want.'

'What kind of defence?'

'Well, you know I told you that I asked him the normal questions as to any previous claims he'd made, and that he said he'd never made any claims.'

'Yes,' said Mr Waite, beginning to look hopeful.

'Well—I've found out that twenty years ago he made a claim for twenty pounds in respect of a car accident.'

'Splendid, splendid,' said Mr Waite. 'Good work.'

'It's nothing of the sort,' said Miss Clinch. 'It's a bloody disgrace to put up a defence like that.'

'But it's in the policy,' said Mr Waite. 'If he makes any untrue statement in answering questions relating to his claim he's had it. Good for you.'

'Good for fiddlesticks,' said Miss Clinch. 'In my view this is a bogus claim, and I mean to prove it, if I can—or at least stop him proving it genuine. But if I'm wrong, to take a point like this is about as shabby as anything I've seen in this racket.'

'It'll save a hundred thousand pounds.'

'I dare say. I don't want to save it that way. Anyway, I don't believe the directors would let you take the point.'

'They mightn't if you weren't so dead sure the claim's a fake.'

'Well,' said Miss Clinch grudgingly, 'it is a help, I suppose, to keep the case going for a bit. But if I don't get anything better by the time we get to trial, I wouldn't like to be counsel for the company when the judge hears the defence he's taking.'

Three months later the case came up for trial before Mr Justice Soames. He was a good lawyer and a fair-minded judge. Indeed he had all the more important judicial qualities bar one. Most judges—before being appointed—are fully aware of this quality which Mr Justice Soames lacked. Indeed, one or two are said on appointment to have had printed a small notice, and to have had it placed facing them on their desk in Court, with 'Shut up' on it. Some judges find keeping silence a difficulty; a few an impossibility. They sit down to try a case, determined never to open their mouths except to deliver judgment. But sooner or later some ambiguity in the words of counsel or a witness compels them to speak, and once the ice has been broken they are soon doing what they had determined not to do. Of course, the too silent judge is not always appreciated by the Bar. Most practitioners like to get an idea of what is going through the mind of the man who is trying the case, and, if he doesn't talk, they can't. On the other hand, no counsel likes the judge who talks more than he does. Some judges can be stopped to some extent by experienced counsel in this way. While the judge is talking he keeps such a deliberate advertised silence with mouth firmly closed that the judge eventually begins to hear his own voice going on and on, and to realize that the advocate—the man who is supposed to be saying something—is absolutely quiet. Less experienced counsel interrupt, with the result that you sometimes get the undignified spectacle of judge and counsel talking at the same time and neither of them listening. This is no way to stop a talkative judge. The only possible defence is a purposeful, starry-eyed, tight-lipped silence. Unfortunately, however, there was no method known to stop Mr Justice Soames. Every method, which did not go beyond the bounds of respect, had been tried, but without success.

Mr Richmond was represented by George Stanmore, and the Positive Insurance Company by Andrew Brent, Q.C. and Albert Wardle. As soon as the case had been called on, Stanmore began to open it.

'May it please your Lordship, this is a claim for a hundred thousand pounds due under a policy of insurance issued by the Defendants.'

'When I was at the Bar,' said Mr Justice Soames, 'I once had a case where the amount sued for was one million pounds. I believe that was a record at the time.'

'If your Lordship pleases,' said Stanmore. 'The policy insured the plaintiff against—among other risks—burglary.'

'I believe it was a burglary policy in the case I was thinking of,' said Mr Justice Soames.

'Remarkable,' whispered Brent. 'He wasn't the burglar as well, I suppose? Ask him.'

'If your Lordship pleases,' said Stanmore. 'The facts are in a small compass and are as follows.'

Stanmore then stated Mr Richmond's case in as short a time as the judge's interruptions would allow. Then he went on:

'The defendant raises two defences only. First he puts the plaintiff to proof of the loss. As to that I shall call before your Lordship the bank manager, the two police officers who were called to the scene of the crime, the doctor who attended my client and also the plaintiff himself. I venture to think that part of the case will not cause your Lordship much difficulty.'

'If it does, that's what I'm here for,' said Mr Justice Soames.

'If your Lordship pleases,' said Stanmore.

'I take it that the defendants are not affirmatively alleging that it was a bogus burglary,' said the judge. 'They just want to know that it wasn't.'

'That is not quite the position, my Lord,' said Stanmore. 'If one may judge from the second defence raised by the defendants, they want to find some excuse for not paying this very large claim. I venture to criticize this second defence to which I am about to refer as one of the most shabby defences your Lordship has ever seen—even from an insurance company.'

'Strong language, Mr Stanmore,' said the judge.

'Called for in this case, my Lord,' said Stanmore. He then told the judge that the defendants' second defence was the accidental mis-statement his client had made to Miss Clinch.

'It is quite true, my Lord, that my client did say to Miss Clinch that he had never made a claim under any policy before; it is quite true that that statement was in fact untrue in that he had once claimed and received twenty pounds under an accident policy. Whatever the legal aspect of that defence may be, how a respectable company can disgrace its profession —I use the words advisedly—can disgrace its profession by

raising such a defence is beyond my comprehension, and if it
were not impertinent of me to speculate on your Lordship's
comprehension, I should venture to say that it was beyond
that too.'

'I gather,' said Mr Justice Soames, 'that you think it is a
good defence.'

'Certainly not, my Lord,' said Stanmore.

'Oh!' said the judge. 'From your vehement attack upon the
merits or what you would call the demerits of the defence, I
rather inferred that you thought it a point of considerable
substance against you. If not, why the heat? I ask myself. I
remember the late Mr Justice Purbright saying something on
the subject. Now, what was it? Oh—yes, I remember: "If
you've all the law and none of the merits go hard for the
corner"—he was a great rugby player you know—"if you've
all the merits and none of the law leave it to the judge. Oddly
enough," he said, "they have a sneaking regard for justice." '

'If your Lordship pleases. Very well, my Lord. In those
circumstances I will content myself with saying that the
defendants are relying upon the fact that my client had forgotten that he had made a claim for twenty pounds in respect
of a car accident twenty years previously—when he was being
asked about a burglary entailing the loss of a hundred thousand
pounds.'

'Much more effective, if I may say so, Mr Stanmore,' said
the judge. 'In the first way you put it, I could hardly see you
for the heat and steam you had generated. Never mind. Don't
let's waste too much time. Will you call your evidence?'

'If your Lordship pleases. With your Lordship's permission
I will call the bank manager first so that, if my friend doesn't
want him to stay and your Lordship agrees, he can be released.
He has rather an important engagement.'

'Certainly, Mr Stanmore. Any order you like. And you're
quite right. We mustn't detain any witness longer than
necessary. Personally I think there should be some scheme
by which witnesses didn't have to spend so much time away

from their work. The time that is wasted in this building is quite deplorable—quite deplorable. If you added it up and translated it into terms of money it would amount to a considerable sum before you finished.'

'If he added up all his interruptions, they'd make quite a tidy sum too,' whispered Brent.

The bank manager then went into the witness box and was sworn.

'Is your full name Albert Smith Trevallic?' asked Stanmore.

'It is.'

'Smith Trevallic?' queried the judge. 'That's an odd combination. Cornish, I presume?'

'Durham, my Lord.'

'I beg your pardon?' said the judge.

'Durham, my Lord,' repeated the bank manager.

'But that can't be,' said the judge. 'No doubt you yourself came from Durham, but your forbears must have come from Cornwall. You know the rhyme, "Tre, Pol and Pen are the Cornish men?"'

'No, my Lord, I'm afraid I don't. We've always lived in Durham.'

'But I assure you, Mr Trevallic, that's quite impossible. This is a subject I do know something about. All the Tre's come from Cornwall.'

'Sit down and have a rest, my dear fellow,' whispered Brent to Stanmore. 'This'll take till lunch.'

'As a matter of fact,' said the witness, 'my grandfather's name was Smith.'

'On one side of the family, no doubt,' said the judge. 'Your mother's possibly?'

'My father's,' began the witness.

'So the Cornish blood is maternal,' said the judge.

'My mother's name was Smith too,' said the witness.

'Well, where does the Trevallic come in?'

'As a matter of fact, my Lord, they happened to be staying in the village of Trevallic for their honeymoon, and they

liked the name and the place so much they changed their
name.'

'Trevallic—Trevallic—I don't remember any Trevallic in
Cornwall,' said the judge.

'It's not in Cornwall, my Lord.'

'Where is it then? Just near the border, I suppose?'

'It's near Durham, my Lord.'

'Now, this is most interesting,' began the judge. 'This means
that there must have been a movement North West from
Cornwall—let me see . . . but I'm interrupting you, Mr
Stanmore—I'm so sorry.'

'Not at all, my Lord,' said Stanmore, 'and do you live at
19 Mardeville Place, W.1?'

'You mean Mandeville Place,' put in the judge.

'No, my Lord. I think it's Mardeville.'

'I've never heard of it,' said the judge. 'It must be a mistake.
Isn't that so?' he asked the witness.

'No, my Lord. It is Mardeville Place.'

'Where exactly is that?' asked the judge.

'Well, my Lord, it's only a small turning. If your Lordship
knows Wigmore Road . . .'

'Wigmore Road? Wigmore Road? You mean Wigmore Street?'

'No, my Lord, Wigmore Road.'

'Where is it near?'

'Well, perhaps your Lordship knows Marylebone Street?'

'Marylebone High Street you mean?'

'No, my Lord, Marylebone Street.'

'Are you sure you don't mean Marylebone Lane?'

'No, my Lord.'

'Well—I've never heard of Marylebone Street. Where is it
exactly?'

'Does your Lordship know Orchard Road?'

'Orchard Street you mean?'

'No, my Lord—Orchard Road; it's not far from Orchard
Street—near Portman Gardens.'

'Square, you mean.'

'No, Gardens, my Lord.'

'This is very odd,' said the judge.

'Well—your Lordship knows Oxford Street.'

'Yes, we're on common ground at last.'

'Well, you know where it runs into Tottenham Court Street?'

'Road you mean.'

'No, Street, my Lord. It's not far from the Road.'

'Never heard of it,' said the judge. 'Any way, you live at Mardeville Street. I suppose a taxi would take me there?'

'No, my Lord.'

'Why on earth not?'

'Well, my Lord, it's a one way street at one end and a cul-de-sac at the other.'

'But that's absurd,' said the judge. 'You must be able to drive down it.'

'Well, my Lord, if you drive past it in a northerly direction it says "no left turn." And if you drive past it in a southerly direction it says "Police Notice" . . .'

'Is there a plan?' began the judge, and then recollected that he was not trying an accident case.

'Come along, Mr Stanmore, this witness has an appointment. We don't want to spend any more time on his name and address, do we?'

'I was just becoming interested,' whispered Stanmore to Brent, and then returned to the witness.

'Are you the manager of the Strand branch of the National County Bank?'

'I am.'

'Is the plaintiff a customer of yours?'

'He is.'

'How long has he been a customer?'

'About seven years.'

'And what sort of an account has it been, Mr Trevallic?'

'Excellent.'

'Now,' began Stanmore . . . but the judge intervened.

'What exactly do you mean by excellent?' he asked.

'A large credit has always been maintained, my Lord.'

'I see,' said the judge. 'I'm afraid I'm not able to maintain a large credit. How would you describe my account?'

'I'm sure it's excellent too, my Lord.'

'Thank you,' said the judge. 'Then what is the criterion of an excellent account?'

'A good customer always maintains an excellent account.'

'Then what is a good customer?' countered the judge.

'A good customer,' replied the witness, 'is a customer who is always to be trusted. Naturally the larger the account the better the bank is pleased. But, apart from credit squeezes, a secured overdraft is very welcome to a bank—provided—and this is the point—provided the customer is to be trusted.'

'You mean, I suppose,' said the judge, 'he always keeps his word and never goes above the agreed limit of his overdraft?'

'Precisely, my Lord.'

'And you say that Mr Richmond, the plaintiff, did all those things?'

'Yes, my Lord.'

'Yes—Mr Stanmore?' said the judge, condescending to put the ball into play again.

'Did Mr Richmond ever have an overdraft?' asked Stanmore.

'Never.'

'But I thought you said,' interrupted the judge—gathering the ball again into his ubiquitous hands—'that the bank did not mind a properly secured overdraft?'

'That is quite true, my Lord.'

'Then I don't understand,' said the judge, 'why Mr Stanmore is claiming such credit for his client never having had an overdraft.'

'My Lord,' began Stanmore . . .

'But don't let's worry about that now,' said the judge. 'Do let's get on with the evidence, or this case will take a week. What are you asking this witness to prove? At present we only know his name and address and that he's a bank manager.'

B

'If your Lordship would allow me to ask a few more questions——' began Stanmore.

'That is what you're there for, Mr Stanmore,' said the judge.

'I was beginning to doubt it,' whispered Stanmore to Brent. 'Thank you, my Lord,' he said aloud to the judge.

'What was the state of the plaintiff's account on the morning of 15th June?'

'He had a hundred and five thousand pounds in credit.'

'Is that not a very large sum to have in a current account?' asked the judge.

'It is, my Lord.'

'Has the plaintiff always maintained such a large credit?'

'It has been large, very large, for some time, but nothing like as large as that. He has recently sold some securities and transferred some money from a deposit account.'

'I see,' said the judge. 'Did he tell you why?'

'Yes, my Lord,' began the witness. 'Mr Richmond told me——'

'No, don't tell me what Mr Richmond said,' interrupted the judge. 'I mustn't ask you that. Mr Brent may, if he wishes. I expect that sounds pretty odd to you, Mr Trevallic?'

'Yes, my Lord.'

'It's one of the rules of evidence, you know. Have you ever read *Pickwick Papers*?'

'Yes, my Lord.'

'Well, no doubt you remember Mr Justice Stareleigh telling Sam Weller that he mustn't say what the soldier said.'

'Yes, my Lord, but——'

'But what, Mr Trevallic?'

'Well, my Lord, if I mustn't say what the soldier said—that is, what Mr Richmond—the soldier in this case—said, how can I say it if Mr Brent asks me and not if your Lordship does?'

'I'm afraid there isn't time for me to instruct you in the rules of evidence. But there are times when Mr Brent couldn't ask you—in fact when no one could. It's often not appreciated

that hearsay is still hearsay, whether it's in cross-examination
or in examination in chief. I don't suppose that means anything
to you, Mr Trevallic?'

'Frankly no, my Lord.'

'Well, that's the answer to your question. Now, Mr Stanmore,
we really must get on. I'm afraid it's partly my fault.'

'Oh, no, my Lord,' protested Stanmore. 'My learned friend
and I must share the blame.'

'Well—don't do it again then,' said the judge pleasantly.

'Now, Mr Trevallic,' said Stanmore, 'do you remember
Mr Richmond calling on you on the afternoon of the 15th
June?'

'I do.'

'For what purpose?'

'To cash a cheque for a hundred thousand pounds.'

'What precautions were taken?' asked the judge. 'It's a very
large sum of money.'

'The money was brought to me in my room,' said the
witness, 'and I personally handed it over to Mr Richmond.'

'How did he take it away?'

'In a large suitcase.'

'I see,' said the judge. 'Was there anyone with him?'

'No, my Lord.'

'How did he take the money—in five pound notes?'

'No, my Lord, in one pound and ten shilling notes.'

'It must have weighed quite a lot.'

'It did, my Lord.'

The judge paused for a moment.

'Has your Lordship finished with the witness?' asked
Stanmore.

'Finished with the witness? Certainly not. Why do you
ask?'

'I wanted to ask him a question, my Lord.'

'Well, of course you may,' said the judge. 'I'm sorry if I
intervened at an inopportune moment.'

'Not at all, my Lord. It was most helpful of your Lordship.

Now, Mr Trevallic, will you answer this question "yes" or "no"—before the money was taken away was there a conversation between you and Mr Richmond?'

'Yes.'

'Did you make any recommendation to the plaintiff?'

'Recommendation?' queried the witness.

Stanmore was bringing the witness to the matter of insurance, but he was not entitled to ask him point blank whether he mentioned insurance. That would be a leading question. He had to squeeze it out of the witness without putting the words into his mouth. Some witnesses take a lot of squeezing.

'Yes—did you recommend anything to Mr Richmond?'

'Recommend?' said the witness again.

'Yes,' said Stanmore.

'My learned friend is not going to lead, I hope,' put in Brent, scenting danger.

'I haven't led the witness in the least,' said Stanmore crossly. It was bad enough not getting what he wanted out of the witness, without leading, and now he was accused of being about to lead. In fact that was exactly what he intended to do. As gently as possible in the first instance.

'Did I recommend anything?' asked the witness again.

'Yes,' repeated Stanmore.

'About what?' asked the witness.

'About anything,' said Stanmore—'the safety of the money for example.'

'Really,' expostulated Brent. 'I object. I particularly asked my friend not to lead.'

'Well, he's asked it now,' said the judge. 'Did you recommend anything about the safety of the money?'

'The safety of the money . . .' The witness hesitated. 'You mean where it was to be kept, I suppose?'

'Well,' said Stanmore, 'was anything said about that?'

It was not what he wanted, but it was better than nothing and, as long as the ball was in play, it was something.

'Well, I asked if he had a safe, and he said "yes." '

'I see,' said Stanmore. 'Was anything else said?'

'Anything else?' queried the witness. 'About what?'

'Now,' warned Brent.

'Please,' said Stanmore. 'My learned friend must keep quiet.'

'Last time I kept quiet you took advantage of it to ask a leading question.'

'Anything else about anything,' said Stanmore to the witness.

'I don't seem to remember anything,' said the witness.

'Think, Mr Trevallic.'

'Now,' said Brent, rather more menacingly.

'Was anything more said about anything?' repeated the witness, puzzled. 'No, I can't recall anything. We discussed the weather, no doubt—but I take it you don't mean that?'

'No, I don't,' snapped Stanmore.

'As a matter of fact . . .' the witness began again.

'Yes?' said Stanmore hopefully.

'Well——' said the witness, apologetically, 'we did talk about cricket, as a matter of fact.'

'Cricket,' said the judge—brightening. 'Are you a cricketer by any chance?'

'Not to play, my Lord, but I follow the game a lot. We were talking about catches, as a matter of fact——'

'The most spectacular catch that I ever saw,' said the judge, 'was at Lords. I remember—but I'm interrupting again. I'm so very sorry. You were saying, Mr Stanmore?'

'Did you discuss anything besides the weather, cricket and the fact that the plaintiff had a safe?'

'No—not so far as I remember,' said the witness. And then added, as though it were an afterthought—'We discussed insurance, of course.'

Stanmore sighed—a mixture of relief and exhaustion.

'And what did you say?'

'I suggested that Mr Richmond should insure the money overnight while at his house.'

'Why did you suggest that?'

'Because I thought it was a risk having all that money.'

'Yes, of course, but why did *you* suggest it?'

'Why did *I* suggest it?'

'Yes.'

'I don't quite understand.'

'Well, as far as you knew—before the subject was mentioned —was the plaintiff going to insure the money?'

'Before the subject was mentioned?'

'Yes.'

'Well, before the subject was mentioned I didn't know.'

'No, of course not, but who raised the subject?'

'I think I did.'

'You *think?*'

'That's what he said,' said Brent, 'and I've written it down.'

'Why do you think you raised it?' asked the judge.

'Because I think I did, my Lord.'

'Yes—you've said so,' said the judge, 'but *why* do you think it?'

'Why?'

'Yes.'

'Because I do, my Lord.'

'So you have said, but why?' persisted the judge.

'I don't know, my Lord.'

'But you must know.'

'But I don't, my Lord,' said the witness. 'I'm very sorry, my Lord,' he added.

'Now look,' said the judge, 'you think you talked about cricket . . .'

'No, my Lord, I know that.'

'Well—just assume you only think you talked about cricket. Why should you think it?'

'I've no idea, my Lord.'

'That's nonsense, Mr Trevallic.'

'I'm sorry, my Lord.'

'It's no use being sorry,' the judge replied. 'Now, look, Mr Trevallic. There is a reason for everything.'

'And that goes for his being on the Bench,' whispered Brent, 'but I can't think what it is.'

'Yes, my Lord,' said the witness obediently.

'If you think that anything happened there must be a reason for your so thinking. For example—the fact that it happened is a reason for thinking it happened. D'you follow so far?'

'Yes,' said the witness unhappily, not following at all.

'Well, now that you understand that, Mr Trevallic, why do you think you raised the subject of insurance?'

'Because I did, my Lord. I mean I do.'

'Now, which is it? You did or you do?'

'Did or do what, my Lord?'

'Mr Trevallic, you must try to help me. I'm sure you are really, but perhaps you'll try a little harder.'

For the moment Mr Trevallic devoutly wished the plaintiff had never had an account with him. He was an excellent bank manager, he was well educated, travelled, played tennis, he had many friends, enjoyed the theatre and cinema—in fact he was an intelligent all-rounder, but this was too much for him. He recollected with some relief that his blood pressure was good.

'Now, listen,' continued the judge. 'I asked you why you think you raised the subject of insurance, and you at first said "because I did"—that would mean because you did raise it . . . the question of insurance—d'you follow me so far?—and then you corrected yourself and said—"I mean I do"—that means you think you raised it because you think you raised it—which is the same thing—it's just repeating the question and doesn't get us any further. Do you still follow?'

'Follow what, my Lord?'

'Follow me.'

The witness said nothing. He was completely out of his depth.

'Well, Mr Trevallic, take your time. Don't hurry over the answer.'

The witness took his time. The clock could be heard ticking
—a sure sign that someone is taking his time.

'Well,' said the judge, 'still thinking for the answer?'

'Yes, my Lord.'

The judge paused and then as it were with a sudden inspira-
tion he said, quite sharply:

'Why?'

'Why what, my Lord?' said the witness, after he had
recovered from the shock.

'Why are you still thinking for the answer?'

'Because you asked me, my Lord.'

'Now, then,' said the judge triumphantly, 'doesn't that start
a train of thought?'

'A train of thought, my Lord?'

'Yes.'

'In what direction, my Lord?'

The judge's patience gave out.

'To Edinburgh via Carlisle and Glasgow,' he snapped.
'Continue with your examination, Mr Stanmore, I've done
all I can.'

'If your Lordship pleases,' said Stanmore. 'Whoever it was
that raised the matter of insurance, Mr Trevallic,' he went on,
'what was done about it?'

'I telephoned our brokers, and an insurance was arranged.'

'As far as you could tell would an insurance have been
arranged if the subject had not been mentioned in your office?'

'I imagine not.'

'And who do you think first raised the subject?'

'I did.'

'Thank you, Mr Trevallic.'

Stanmore sat down. Brent stood up.

'Mr Trevallic,' he began, 'I want you to take your mind
back to the interview with Mr Richmond.'

What is it now? thought the witness.

'I'll do my best,' he said.

'Do you think it possible,' asked Brent, 'that the subject of

insurance was first mentioned by Mr Richmond? Like this, I
mean. Do you think he might have said to you that he wasn't
going to bother to insure the money?'

'I suppose that is possible.'

'And naturally enough, if he had said that, you would have
persuaded him to have it insured?'

'Quite possibly.'

Miss Clinch, sitting in Court next to Mr Waite, turned and
looked at him with an air of triumph.

'I dare say,' whispered Mr Waite, 'but a fat lot of good it'll
do you.'

'This is all very interesting,' said the judge, 'but what has
all this got to do with the case?'

Mr Waite looked at Miss Clinch.

'My learned friend led evidence to show that insurance was
first mentioned by the manager,' said Brent.

'I dare say he did,' said the judge, 'but I didn't know then
what it had got to do with it.'

'Your Lordship let him ask the question.'

'I dare say I did, but I have to leave it to counsel to some
extent, don't I? I can't interrupt all the time, can I?'

'He gives a very good imitation of it,' whispered Stanmore
to Brent.

'What is the relevance, Mr Brent? This is a claim under a
policy. The plaintiff says he's lost a hundred thousand pounds
and claims it from the defendants. You say—first prove your
loss and secondly, if he does prove it, you seek to rely upon
what I'm bound to say at first blush seems to be a pretty
discreditable defence. Indeed, I should have thought that
blush was not at all an inappropriate word to use in connection
with it.'

'My Lord,' began Brent.

'Well, now,' went on the judge, 'I don't see what the question who first suggested insurance has got to do with it. There's
no doubt a policy was issued. Wouldn't it be better to let
Mr Trevallic go to his appointment, and let the plaintiff come

into the box? He's the man you want to see. Did he really have a burglary or not? That's the really important point, isn't it?'

'Yes, indeed, my Lord.'

'And while we're on the subject, if the plaintiff does satisfy me that he has had a loss of a hundred thousand pounds, do you really want to rely on the mean little defence referred to by Mr Stanmore?'

'Those are my instructions, my Lord.'

'You could take fresh instructions, Mr Brent. Your clients have a reputation, you know—on the whole a very good one indeed. It's not often they take points like these—seriously, I mean. Oh—yes, I know if they're not sure of a claim they sometimes put them in in the first instance—but they don't often persist in them—not in my experience—and this one really is rather shameful. Wouldn't you like to take fresh instructions, Mr Brent?'

'If your Lordship pleases,' said Brent.

He spoke to his solicitor.

'Well,' he said, 'I told you this would happen. What about it? It's a rotten point, anyway. I never knew why they insisted on taking it.'

'I'll speak to someone on the phone,' said the solicitor. 'I'm not going to drop it because old Soames is shouting at you. I'm going to get instructions.'

'My client will take further instructions,' said Brent to the judge.

'Very well,' said the judge, 'but if I were the defendant I'd be very sorry to take a point like this. Now, what about Mr Trevallic, he wants to get back to Cornwall—Durham, I mean.'

At that moment there was a slight noise at the back of the Court as someone came in.

'Silence,' called the usher.

'Good gracious,' said Mr Tewkesbury, who had just arrived in a somewhat exalted state, 'I've come to the wrong bar.'

'Silence,' called the usher again.

The judge looked towards the door and recognized Mr Tewkesbury. He glared in his direction.

Mr Tewkesbury came a little unsteadily towards the row behind Stanmore and eventually settled himself there. Stanmore suddenly became aware of his presence—not because he had heard him—he had been looking up a point in his brief during the slight disturbance—nor because he had looked round and seen him—but because of the blast of hot whisky fumes which suddenly assailed him.

'How's it going?' asked Mr Tewkesbury.

'Silence,' called the usher.

'Must be allowed to instruct Counsel,' said Mr Tewkesbury. 'Solicitor's privilege.'

'Mr Stanmore,' said the judge, 'will you ask your client to speak less audibly when he instructs you, please?'

'If your Lordship pleases.'

Stanmore turned round and, facing Mr Tewkesbury, received the full undiluted gale—force eight.

'For Heaven's sake be quiet,' he said.

'Glad to see you, Mr Stanmore,' said Mr Tewkesbury, rather more quietly. 'Come out and have one.'

'Go and have one yourself,' said Stanmore.

'Good idea,' said Mr Tewkesbury. 'Don't mind if I do. Keep it going till I come back.'

Meanwhile Mr Richmond went into the witness box, and Mr Trevallic went to keep his appointment. The judge allowed the plaintiff to give his name and address without interruption, but the rest of his evidence in chief consisted of the judge asking the questions with Stanmore a poor second. The witness himself gave his evidence well and described the burglary convincingly. Brent then started to cross-examine him.

'Were you rendered unconscious by the blow?'

'Not entirely.'

'What do you mean by that?' asked the judge. 'Either you were unconscious or you were not.'

'I did not fully lose consciousness, my Lord, but I was dazed.'

'A very good answer,' said the judge. 'Much the same as when I had concussion once playing rugby. Indeed I played through the rest of the game but it felt unreal. Yes—dazed is the word.'

'And how long do you think you remained in that condition?' continued Brent.

'What does it matter?' said the judge. 'You're not suggesting that he wasn't struck on the head?'

'I'm entitled to test his story, my Lord.'

'I should have thought the doctor was the best witness to ask about the injury. He is being called, I understand.'

'Does your Lordship then rule that I may not ask the plaintiff about the injury to which he has referred?'

'I rule nothing of the sort,' said the judge, 'but there's no jury, you know. It's *my* decision you wish to obtain.'

'Then I propose to ask some more questions on the subject, my Lord,' said Brent.

'By all means,' said the judge, 'if you think it will do any good.'

'Now, Mr Richmond,' began Brent—but the judge was too quick for him.

'Forgive me, Mr Brent,' he said. 'Tell me, Mr Richmond, on what part of the head were you struck?'

'On the top, my Lord, towards the forehead.'

'You'll forgive my mentioning it, but in view of the fact that you are almost bald it must have been painful.'

'It was, my Lord.'

'Did it bleed?'

'Yes, my Lord.'

'Did the doctor see the blood?'

'Yes, my Lord.'

'Did he attend to your injury?'

'Yes, my Lord.'

'Could you recognize either of the men again?'

'I doubt it, my Lord, in view of their disguise.'

'Did you ring the police as soon as you were free?'

'I did, my Lord.'

'How long did it take you to get free?'

'It seemed a long time, my Lord, but I suppose it may have been half an hour or more.'

'You say the wireless was on at the time?'

'Yes, my Lord.'

'Who had turned it on?'

'I had, my Lord.'

'Why?'

'I find it a soporific, my Lord.'

'Somewhat expensive if it's on all night?'

'Less expensive than getting into the habit of taking sleeping pills.'

'Very wise, Mr Richmond,' said the judge. 'Yes, Mr Brent,' he said encouragingly. 'Your next question?'

Miss Clinch did not enjoy her lunch that day.

'Can't you get an adjournment or something?' she said to Mr Waite. 'I believe I shall find something if I can have more time. That chap's a crook if ever there was one.'

'The judge doesn't seem to think so,' said Mr Waite.

'The judge!' said Miss Clinch contemptuously. 'He's made up his mind already.'

'Well, I agree that he should appear to wait a bit,' said Mr Waite, 'but can you blame him on the evidence? There's everything in Richmond's favour and nothing in ours—only your confounded intuition. I tell you, Miss Clinch, it is entirely due to our tremendous opinion of you that this case has been fought. You've never been wrong up to date.'

'I'm not wrong now.'

'Well, I'm afraid Mr Justice Soames is very shortly going to say you are.'

'True enough,' said Miss Clinch, 'but he says so much it can't all be right.'

It was not long, however, before the defendants—in the face

of Mr Justice Soames' pointed remarks—threw their hand
in.

'I'm sorry, Miss Clinch,' said Mr Scale, their solicitor who
was a large friendly man—'but there it is. You can't expect
our clients to take any more punishment. They've got their
position in the City to think of. But thank you for all your
good work.'

'Thank my billowing aunt,' said Miss Clinch. She was not
pleased.

CHAPTER FIVE

Miss Clinch's Discovery

THE defendants having withdrawn their defence and consented to judgment there was nothing left to them but to pay. And this they did. But only a few days after they had done so, Miss Clinch burst into Mr Waite's office.

'I knew I was right. You must get that money back.'

'What have you found out?'

'Enough to land Mr Richmond where he belongs.'

'Not really? Tell me.'

Miss Clinch told him: 'It was obvious to me almost from the outset that a frontal attack was no good. He'd done all the right things, sent for a doctor and called the police, been to the bank manager and so forth and so on. So an outflanking movement was necessary, but that takes time and I wasn't given enough.'

'But what have you found out?'

'You must allow me the pleasure of telling you in my own way,' said Miss Clinch firmly. 'To continue,' she went on, 'I am not a believer in first offences.'

'What on earth do you mean by that?'

'Simply that I don't believe people are found out the first time. Oh, I know everyone has to pretend it's a first offence. "A person of unblemished character," they say. "Can't think what made me do it," says the shoplifter when caught for the first time. What made her do it that time was the fact that she'd been doing it successfully for years, or months anyway. Oh—of course—she had to start . . . there was in fact a first

offence—but very few people have the bad luck to be caught
first time. Anyway, that's what I believe. I can't prove it, of
course, in most cases, but I've no doubt about it in my own
mind. Well, now, I said to myself, if, as I believe, Mr Richmond
is trying to defraud the insurance company, it won't be the
first time he's tried it on.'

'But he's got no record—except that ridiculous twenty
pound accident claim.'

'Hasn't he?' said Miss Clinch.

'But if he has, why on earth——'

'I asked for more time, Mr Waite,' said Miss Clinch, 'and
if you'd got it for me I could have told you before. Of course,
he hasn't any record in his own name. I've been making
enquiries about *other* names. That's why it's taken such a long
time. And I've found three cases of what may fairly be termed
honest-to-God fraudulent claims. Much smaller amounts, of
course, but plainly fraudulent. Indeed, when the fraud was
discovered, the police were notified in each case—but the bird
had flown. He's never been found.'

'Then I don't follow——'

'Do be patient, Mr Waite. All these three cases were single
insurances by one man. The name in one case was Cholmeley,
in another Urquhart, and in the third Smith. Now, did you
notice anything about Mr Richmond? Well—this isn't a quiz,
so I'll tell you. He's bald, isn't he?'

'He is.'

'And did you notice that he had a limp?'

'Yes.'

'I have discovered that Mr Cholmeley, Mr Urquhart and
Smith were all bald and all lame.'

'But can they be identified as Richmond?'

'I don't know,' said Miss Clinch. 'If we're lucky, yes, but
I'm quite prepared to assume that they can't be.'

'Now, really, Miss Clinch, you're not seriously saying that,
because Richmond happens to be bald and lame and these
other three men . . . or no, I've got your point—this other one

man who used three different names—is bald and lame, he is the same person? Really, you're letting your enthusiasm go to your head.'

'Have you finished?' asked Miss Clinch. 'May I without disrespect say that you are giving an extraordinarily good imitation of Mr Justice Soames? You must take me for a very considerable fool if you think that my positive identification— yes . . . I said positive identification—rests on baldness and lameness.'

'But I thought you said you were prepared to assume there would be no identification.'

'No personal identification, I meant. No one who could say, looking at Richmond, "He is Cholmeley," or "He is Urquhart," or "He is Smith," or any one or more of them. Yes, I said that. But all these three gentlemen sent letters and so did Mr Richmond, and, Mr Waite, *they all used the same typewriter*.'

'Are you sure?' said Mr Waite, after a pause while he recovered from the shock which Miss Clinch was delighted to have given him.

'In view of the fact that my name is mud in this office,' said Miss Clinch, 'I went to an expert myself—though anyone could really tell from looking at them that they must have been typed on the same machine. I've got them here.'

She brought out four letters.

'You see how the "e" is always just above the line in each case?'

Mr Waite looked. He saw.

'And the "t" runs into the "l"?'

Mr Waite saw again.

'Well, I didn't want you to take my word for it. Here's the report. It's a true bill. Shall I get on to Scotland Yard?'

CHAPTER SIX

Mr Tewkesbury at Work

Not long after Miss Clinch's discovery, Brent and Stanmore were lunching together.

'Forgive my saying so, old boy,' said Brent, 'but how can you stomach old Tewkesbury as a client? He nearly blew me out of Court and I was well away from him.'

'A fair question,' said Stanmore. 'I wouldn't in the normal way, of course. His instructions are meaningless, he seldom keeps an appointment—though that is an advantage really— and no one could trust him an inch. Still, as he's so continuously drunk now, I doubt if he's capable of doing anything deliberately dishonest—simply because he's not capable of doing anything deliberately at all, except lifting a glass.'

'Then why did you appear for him? I was amazed.'

'I'll tell you. It was his client. I've done one or two things for him in the past, when he had other solicitors, and he seems a very decent chap. So I didn't very well see how I could refuse, and I couldn't really tell him to change his solicitor. Though why a chap like Richmond goes to Tewkesbury beats me.'

'I see,' said Brent. 'Well, don't pass this on, but I fancy you may be appearing for your friend Mr Richmond again very shortly.'

'Oh?'

'Yes—and you may have to revise your ideas about his character a bit. Possibly it'll explain why he goes to Tewkesbury.'

'What's it all about?'

'Well, I can't tell you now, old boy. But you'll soon learn. That's if you do any criminal work.'

'What!'

Brent looked at his watch.

'I fancy they may be executing the warrant just about now.'

Twenty-four hours later Mr Richmond was arrested and shortly afterwards released on bail. On his release he went straight to see Mr Tewkesbury. Something must have gone wrong, for he was rather more sober than usual.

'Good morning, my dear sir,' he said cordially. 'Have you by any chance lost another hundred thousand pounds?'

'Mr Tewkesbury,' said Richmond. 'A dreadful thing has happened. There's been a terrible mistake. I've been charged with attempted fraud.'

'Attempted, my dear sir? That must be bitter. Now, if it had been the hundred thousand pounds—at least you've had that—but attempted, attempted—may I offer my condolences?'

'It is the hundred thousand pounds.'

Mr Tewkesbury's face brightened.

'Ah, that's better. At least you've tasted the sweets. That's something. And you ought to be able to put it away somewhere, my dear sir, until you come out. You've relieved my mind a great deal, my dear sir. You had me really worried at first.'

'Mr Tewkesbury,' said Mr Richmond, 'I am entirely innocent of this charge. I would have you know that.'

Mr Tewkesbury put his finger alongside his nose and winked.

'My dear sir, all my clients are innocent—as innocent as the day is long. Let me see—the last got seven years . . . or was it five?—no matter, a considerable term—but it was a gross miscarriage of justice, sir, a gross miscarriage. We took the matter to the Court of Criminal Appeal, sir, I would have you know. The Lord Chief Justice himself presided. And at least I may say he disagreed with the judge at the trial.'

'Your client got off on appeal, then?'

'Well, not exactly,' said Mr Tewkesbury. 'They increased the sentence. But I still maintain his innocence. And so does he—from a distance—the Isle of Wight, I think, at the moment. And then another one, sir, three years he got for a first offence —a first offence. It was monstrous, sir. He too was absolutely innocent. I would stake my entire professional reputation on it, sir. In that case it was perjury that did it, gross perjury. All the witnesses for the prosecution perjured themselves disgracefully; my client alone told the truth. But how is one to prove it, sir? That was our difficulty. One man's word against ten. I had the best counsel, sir, a Mr Frith Wyndham, sir, I expect you know him. He thundered away at the jury, sir, for so long that eventually the judge made him sit down. And he went on thundering while seated, until the judge stopped that too. And would you believe it, sir, the jury—without leaving the box— found my client guilty. But what can you do, sir, what can you do? I can only hope no perjury is committed in your case, sir.'

'Perhaps I'd better tell you about it, Mr Tewkesbury—or better still, could we have a conference with Mr Stanmore?'

Mr Tewkesbury hesitated for a moment. He was considering whether he had paid Stanmore's fees. It was not his habit to pay counsel unless absolutely compelled to do so, and he realized that it was sometimes difficult to obtain a conference with counsel when he had just been bilked. He had, however, a feeling that in this particular case he had been weak enough to yield to the blandishments of Stanmore's clerk.

'I wonder,' he said aloud.

'Wonder what?' asked Mr Richmond.

'Nothing, my dear sir,' said Mr Tewkesbury, 'nothing of any moment. Let me think,' he added. 'Miss Winter,' he called a few moments later.

Miss Winter came in.

'Did you call, sir?' she asked.

'I want the box where I keep counsels' receipts. Come along . . . Mr Richmond's a busy man.'

Miss Winter went out, and returned shortly afterwards with a box-file labelled 'Counsels' Receipts.' It was empty.

'That's odd,' said Mr Tewkesbury. 'I felt sure——'

Mr Tewkesbury was quite right in feeling sure. Paying counsel was such a rare event in his life that, on the infrequent occasions when he did so, the pain made a deep impression. In the course of years he had been to nearly every set of chambers in the Temple until his credit gave out. The reason he could still find counsel to brief was that there were always young men who wanted experience and were prepared to risk not being paid, and there were always old men who lived on hope and who, if necessary, were prepared to listen to the sound of their own voices for nothing. Then occasionally— very occasionally—when there was no other way, he paid in advance. Stanmore's clerk knew all about Mr Tewkesbury, and would no more have thought of giving him credit than of forgetting to charge clerk's fees. On this particular occasion, when Mr Tewkesbury had lurched into Stanmore's chambers, the clerk had not been at all pleased to see him.

'I have come,' said Mr Tewkesbury, with alcoholic dignity, 'I have come to enquire whether Mr Stanmore of counsel is prepared to accept instructions from my firm.'

'Cheque with brief,' the clerk had said bluntly.

'The labourer is—in this case,' Mr Tewkesbury had replied, '—worthy of his hire. Although I do not much care for the insin . . . the insinu . . . the suggestion you make that Mr Stanmore's fees will not be paid at all—unless paid in advance —nevertheless in the special circumstances of this case I have been put in the necessary funds to comply with your most offensive requirements, Mr Spring. Most offensive require- ments—I repeat.'

'Is it the client's cheque or yours?' the clerk demanded.

'Which would you prefer?'

For once Mr Spring was at a loss for an answer. What he did not know about the ways of solicitors like Mr Tewkesbury was not worth knowing. In the usual way he would never take the lay client's cheque, but in this case it might not know its way back to the drawer as well or as quickly as Mr Tewkesbury's.

'Who's the client?' he had asked. 'Do we know him?'

'Do you know him, sir? Do you know him? He especially asked for Mr Stanmore. Otherwise—may I say without offence —or indeed with—that I should not have found my way to a place where I am treated with such scant courtesy. To be asked for the fee in advance is an insult, Mr Spring, an insult.'

'It's an insult with which you're pretty well acquainted, Mr Tewkesbury, if I may say so.'

'You may not say so, Mr Spring, you may certainly not say so. When I used to brief Sir Desmond Drinkwater . . .'

'When you briefed Sir Desmond you were dreaming, Mr Tewkesbury. Let's see the cheque, anyway. If you want to take offence and go elsewhere, that suits me fine.'

'It would be undignified,' Mr Tewkesbury had said, 'to retort in the vernacular, but may I say with all respect that, were it not for my client's express instructions, I should tell you and Mr Stanmore to go—to go and chase yourselves— yes, sir, chase yourselves—and I don't mean chase.'

But this conversation had almost faded from Mr Tewkesbury's mind by the time he had his interview with Mr Richmond. He had forgotten, too, that as a final gesture he had lit a cigarette with Mr Stanmore's receipt before leaving his chambers.

CHAPTER SEVEN

Mr Tewkesbury at Play

IN due course the case against Mr Richmond came on for its preliminary hearing before a Metropolitan magistrate. The Director of Public Prosecutions had briefed Brent and a junior, while Mr Richmond was again represented by Stanmore. The magistrate was Mr Temple. Brent and Stanmore arrived in plenty of time and had to wait while the overnight charges were dealt with.

'Your client not here yet?' said Brent. 'That must be a relief to you.'

'It is,' said Stanmore. 'There are hundreds of efficient and respectable solicitors. Why on earth Richmond has to pick on Tewkesbury I can't fathom.'

'D'you really mean that?' asked Brent, 'or are you acting the little innocent?'

'Of course I mean it.'

'Well, don't you think it possible that your engaging client wants a solicitor who'll do anything for him or who is too drunk to know what he's doing?'

'I hope he didn't come to me for the same reason,' said Stanmore.

'My dear chap, that's his only mistake—to come to you. If he were innocent he couldn't do better than brief you, my dear fellow, but, as he's guilty as he can be, he ought to have gone to one of the less scrupulous members of our order.'

'I don't agree with you about him at all. I still think he's a very decent chap. He's the victim of coincidence.'

'Coincidence my foot,' said Brent. 'However—as our old friend Grimes would say—we shall see, my dear fellow, we shall see.'

At that moment the gaoler called out:

'Charge No. 14, your Worship. Mister Tewkesbury.'

As Mr Tewkesbury was being ushered into the dock, he caught Stanmore's eye and said:

'Be with you in a moment, my dear sir.'

'Why "Mr"?' asked the clerk. 'What's his Christian name?'

'Gave it as Mister,' said the gaoler.

Mr Tewkesbury winked at Stanmore, endeavouring to indicate in one wink that it was a brilliant idea to preserve his dignity in that manner.

'You're charged,' said the clerk, 'with being found drunk and incapable in a public place, to wit Orange Street. Are you guilty or not guilty?'

Mr Tewkesbury ignored the clerk, and looked above him to the magistrate.

'Before we deal with this trumpery little matter,' he said, 'may I ask your Worship a personal question?'

'No,' said the magistrate.

'Thank you,' said Mr Tewkesbury. 'The question is whether I briefed you when you were at the Bar. If so, you might be biassed in my favour.'

'Biassed is fair enough,' whispered Brent to Stanmore.

'I briefed all the more important criminal counsel,' went on Mr Tewkesbury, 'so I fancy your Worship must have come under my patronage at one time or another.'

The magistrate spoke to the clerk.

'Is he still drunk?' he asked in an undertone.

'No more than usual,' said the clerk.

'Why doesn't the Law Society do something about him?'

'They've never found him drunk in charge of a case so far. It isn't professional misconduct to be found dead drunk on the pavement.'

The magistrate sighed.

'Any objection by the police to my trying this case?' he asked.

'None at all, your Worship,' said the constable who was in charge of the case.

'That's uncommonly handsome of you,' said Mr Tewkesbury. 'Uncommonly handsome. This officer should go far.'

'Be quiet, please,' said the magistrate. 'Do you plead guilty or not guilty?'

'What a question, if I may say so,' said Mr Tewkesbury. 'I'm a solicitor of the Supreme Court, admitted in 1920, served my articles with——'

'Guilty or not guilty?' said the clerk—loudly and firmly.

'I was talking to the magistrate,' said Mr Tewkesbury.

'Look,' said the magistrate, 'if you don't plead one way or the other, and stop this nonsense, I shall remand you in custody for a week.'

'But I'm engaged in a case, your Worship. Mr Stanmore of counsel is instructed by me.'

'Is that so, Mr Stanmore?' asked the magistrate.

'Yes, sir,' said Stanmore.

'I suppose you wouldn't care to instruct Mr Stanmore to appear for you now,' suggested the magistrate. He realized that, if left to himself, Mr Tewkesbury might keep his own little case going for an hour, and while Mr Tewkesbury was considering his answer the magistrate scribbled on a piece of paper—'For Heaven's sake do,' and gave it to the clerk to hand it to Stanmore.

'The labourer,' said Mr Tewkesbury, 'is worthy of his hire and, to tell you the truth, I haven't got it on me.'

'How much was found on him?' enquired the magistrate of the constable.

'No money, sir,' said the constable.

'Never carry money about with me, sir,' explained Mr Tewkesbury. 'This case shows how right I am. I might have been robbed while I was asleep.'

'Then you plead guilty?' asked the clerk, hopefully.

'I plead nothing of the kind.'

'But you say yourself you were asleep, and you were found on the pavement.'

'The Queen's Highway, sir. No offence to be asleep thereon. Charged with being drunk thereon. Very different—very different indeed. Drunk!' he said scornfully, and looked at Stanmore to indicate what a ridiculous charge it was.

'Very well, then, not guilty,' said the clerk. 'Take the oath, officer, please.'

The officer, having sworn swiftly and surely as to the quality of the evidence he was about to give, cleared his throat and began:

'At 2·30 a.m. this morning, your Worship, I was proceeding along Orange Street on beat duty when I saw the accused lying on the pavement. I leaned over to see what was the matter and the accused said——' The officer paused and looked at his note-book. 'The accused said,' he went on, ' "take your feet off the pillow." I picked him up but he was unable to stand. His breath smelled strongly of alcohol. I arrested him and conveyed him to the police station. On the way the accused made a number of incoherent remarks, which I could not properly catch. At the station he was charged and in reply to the charge he said——' The witness again looked at his notebook, and then continued:

'He said: "Do noble deeds, not dream them all day long." That's the case, your Worship.'

Mr Tewkesbury looked approvingly at the witness.

'And can you tell me where that particular quotation comes from?' he asked.

'No, sir,' said the constable.

'What does it matter?' said the magistrate.

'What does it matter, sir, what does it matter? It matters a great deal. I am charged with being drunk and—laughable as it may sound—incapable.' Here Mr Tewkesbury gave what he thought was a merry laugh. 'Is it likely that in such a condition

I should quote correctly from . . . now who would you say it was from, sir?'

'Don't be impertinent,' said the magistrate.

Mr Tewkesbury smiled encouragingly, as a master would look at a promising pupil who had just missed the right answer.

'A good many people don't know, sir,' he said. 'Indeed, even my own counsel, a very learned scholar, if I may say so, probably doesn't know. Do you, sir?' and he looked enquiringly towards Stanmore—who in turn looked apologetically at the magistrate.

'Now, look, Mr Tewkesbury,' said the magistrate. 'I have a lot of cases to try and I'm not going to let you waste the time of the Court with ridiculous questions. If you've anything sensible to ask, ask it. The officer says you were drunk *and* incapable. Ask him about that if you want to.'

'Very well, sir,' said Mr Tewkesbury solemnly. 'Let me ask you this, officer, *nunc pro tunc*, if you know what that means.'

The officer looked puzzled.

'What I mean, officer, is that I am asking you a question *now* about something which happened *then*. You did science at school, no doubt, instead of classics—but never mind. Well, now, officer, why do you say I was drunk?'

'Because you couldn't stand and your breath smelled strongly of alcohol.'

'Anything else?'

'You talked incoherently.'

'You mean you couldn't understand what I said?'

'Yes.'

Mr Tewkesbury looked at the magistrate.

'A very different thing from incoherence, sir, as I have just demonstrated with my *nunc* and *tunc*.'

As the magistrate seemed unimpressed, Mr Tewkesbury returned to the witness.

'Perhaps,' he said, 'I talked a language you couldn't understand. You know no Latin, I gather?'

'No, sir.'

'Well, officer, can you swear'—Mr Tewkesbury paused dramatically and raised his hand—'can you swear, officer, with that standard of truth you so recently undertook to observe, that I did not speak in Latin?'

'Apart from the words I understood, sir, it might have been anything.'

'Then, officer,' said Mr Tewkesbury triumphantly, 'it might have been Latin.'

'Yes, sir.'

'Or Greek?'

'Yes, sir.'

'And you thought that, because I talked Latin or Greek, I was drunk. Do you now realize the horrible mistake you have made? Why, at this rate half the masters in our public schools could be charged with being drunk.'

The constable said nothing.

Mr Tewkesbury repeated his question:

'Do you now realize your horrible mistake?'

'I didn't make a mistake, sir.'

'Oh, you did not?' said Mr Tewkesbury—rather more menacingly. 'Tell me, then, what does this mean—*interest reipublicae ut sit finis litium?*'

'It means in this case,' interposed the magistrate, 'that, unless you confine your questions to material ones, I shall remand this case for a week. It's really too bad,' he said, quietly to his clerk, 'something ought to be done about it. I shall write to the Law Society.'

'With regard to the smell of alcohol,' continued Mr Tewkesbury—and then paused. 'I take it,' he went on to the magistrate, 'your Worship considers that material?'

'Most material.'

'I am obliged to you, sir. And I assume you agree with that too, officer?'

'Yes, sir.'

'Then we are all agreed,' said Mr Tewkesbury, 'about this most material smell of alcohol.'

Again he paused and looked wistful, as though wishing he could smell some in the dock.

'Could you say what kind of alcohol you smelled, officer?'

'I couldn't be sure, sir. I think it was whisky.'

'But you're not certain, officer, eh, officer—you're not certain?'

'Not absolutely, sir.'

'Well, officer, would it surprise you to learn that for years I have drunk nothing else except whisky?'

'No, sir, it would not surprise me.'

'Then we're agreed again. Now, officer, listen carefully to this next question, and don't answer it if you're not certain. Are you aware that if a person has drunk whisky over a considerable number of years he is, luckily enough, if I may say so, perpetually surrounded by that lovely aroma—or, as you say more coarsely, smell?'

'I don't know, sir.'

'Very well then, officer. Would you agree that a person may smell of whisky and not be drunk?'

'Yes, sir.'

'Now, officer, I have thee on the hip. One of the reasons you say I was drunk was because I smelled of whisky. But now you admit that a person may so smell and not be drunk. Ergo —if you'll forgive my classicism—you can eliminate smell from your reasons. There are now left only two. And the first is— you say I could not stand. Is that correct?'

'Yes, sir.'

'Did it occur to you that I might be tired?'

'Many people are tired,' interposed the magistrate, 'but they don't lie down in the street.'

'Did you see me lie down in the street, officer?'

'No, sir.'

'Then I might have slipped and fallen just before you found me?'

'You appeared to have been there some time, sir.'

'How can you say that, officer? How far away from me were you when you first saw me?'

'About ten yards, sir.'

'Then I might have fallen when you were twelve yards away?'

'You were quite motionless, sir.'

'How long does it take you to walk twelve yards?'

'A few seconds, sir.'

'Then, for all you know, I may have fallen, tripped or slipped a few seconds before you found me?'

'It is possible, sir.'

'And the shock of falling may have made me unsteady on my legs, may it not?'

'Not like you were, sir.'

'And why not, officer?' thundered Mr Tewkesbury. 'Have you medical as well as constabulary qualifications?'

'No, sir.'

'Then can you say how shock affects everyone?'

'No, sir.'

'Then you can't say that, if a man falls down, the shock might not make him unsteady when he gets up?'

'You weren't unsteady, sir. You couldn't stand.'

'So you say, officer,' said Mr Tewkesbury, 'so you say. When the learned magistrate has heard the whole of this case, I shall ask him to take a different view. *Falsa demonstratio non nocet*—if you follow me—but, of course, you don't. I'm sorry.'

'Any more questions?' asked the magistrate brusquely.

'Indeed, sir,' beamed Mr Tewkesbury, 'I am only *in limine*— on the threshold, sir. Tell me, officer, have you ever known a person with concussion of the brain?'

'I'm not sure that I have, sir.'

'Well—you know, do you not, that if a person is struck on the head he may talk unintelligibly for a time?'

'I believe so, sir.'

'Is it not possible that, when I fell just before you came on the scene, I struck my head?'

'I saw no marks, sir.'

'Did you look for any?'

'I can't say that I did, sir.'

'On the hip again, officer. Hip and thigh, one might say. Then you can't say I wasn't struck on the head.'

'You didn't complain of it, sir.'

'But you yourself said I said things you couldn't understand.'

'Yes, sir.'

'Well, might I not have been complaining that I had been struck on the head?'

'I suppose it's possible, but it didn't sound like that, sir.'

'And what, may I ask, did it sound like?'

'A lot of gibberish, sir.'

'But Latin and Greek sound to you like gibberish, officer, don't they? If I say to you βρεκεκεκὲξ κοὰξ κοάξ, does that sound like Latin, or gibberish to you?'

'I don't know, sir.'

'Then it might be Latin?'

'Yes, sir.'

'Or gibberish?'

'Yes, sir.'

'His Worship will confirm to you that it is in fact Greek— I hope. And it comes, officer, from the chorus in Aristophanes' Frogs. Can you swear that I was not reciting Aristophanes?'

'There seemed to be English words mixed up in it, sir. I caught a word here and there, but it didn't make sense.'

'Perhaps I was translating word by word for your benefit, officer.'

'It didn't sound as though you were translating, sir.'

'And how do I sound when I'm translating?'

'You needn't answer that question, officer,' said the magistrate. 'Are you sure you heard him ask you to take your feet off the pillow?'

'Yes, sir, when I first started to lift him.'

'May I not have said—"Steady with your feet, you careless fellow?" '

'No, sir.'

'You have large feet, have you not?'

'Quite large, sir.'

'And you were very close to me, were you not?'

'Yes, sir.'

'If I thought you were going to tread on me, and if I'd just bumped my head, it would not have been an unreasonable thing to say, would it officer?'

'You didn't say it, sir.'

'Is your hearing very good, officer?'

'It's up to standard, sir.'

Mr Tewkesbury whispered a few words.

'Now then, officer, what did I say then?'

'I don't know, sir.'

'Might it have been—look out for your feet, you careless fellow?'

'It might have been anything, sir.'

'Then the answer's yes. Did you hear what I said quite plainly when you picked me up?'

'Yes, sir.'

'Then my speech was plain?'

'Plain enough, sir, when you said that.'

'When a person is drunk, his speech is usually described as slurred. Mine was plain?'

'It was slurred, sir, but I could make out what you said.'

'Either it was plain or it was slurred. Just now you said it was plain. D'you want to go back on that?'

'I said I could hear that particular sentence plainly, but your speech was slurred and otherwise quite unintelligible.'

'Unless it was in Greek, officer?'

'There was no need to speak to him in Greek,' said the magistrate. 'He was an English policeman. Sober people talk to them in English.'

'But not necessarily if, as the officer has sworn, I had just fallen down and struck my head, sir.'

'The officer has sworn nothing of the sort,' said the magistrate. 'I've really had enough of this for one day. Why, I suppose there's the doctor still to call, and I imagine you'll be all night with him.'

'Let the night come,' said Mr Tewkesbury, 'before we praise the day.'

'I'm going to remand you for a week. I'm sorry for the doctor, but it can't be helped. I'll never get half through the list if we go on with this. In the circumstances I shall allow you bail in your own recognizances. Are you worth ten pounds when all your just debts are paid?'

'It's a nice point,' said Mr Tewkesbury, 'but I hope so. It all depends on what are just debts.'

'He's thinking of counsels' fees,' said Brent to Stanmore.

'Don't you believe it,' said Stanmore, 'he only thinks of them when he's made to pay them.'

So Mr Tewkesbury was remanded on bail and eventually Mr Richmond's case was called on. The magistrate devoted an hour to it, and it was then adjourned for another week. After a few more adjournments he was eventually committed for trial to the Old Bailey, and then, some two months after he had received the £100,000 from the insurance company, his trial began.

Before it began, however, an unsuccessful attempt was made by the insurance company to get back the £100,000. They had consented to judgment being given against them, and although they now alleged fraud this was being disputed by Mr Richmond, and the only course they could take was to bring an action to set aside the judgment. There was no chance of this being heard before the criminal proceedings. The company did indeed try to persuade a judge to order Mr Richmond to bring the money into court pending the hearing of the action. But this attempt was simply defeated by Mr Richmond —who swore that he had already lost all the money by trying to double it in four large bets with a bookmaking company whose name he gave. Miss Clinch was wilder than ever, but she comforted herself with two thoughts—first that she had

C

been right, and secondly that Mr Richmond would in due course get his deserts. The possibility that he really had lost the money to a bookmaker she dismissed as lightly as she had dismissed the possibility that he really had been robbed.

CHAPTER EIGHT

The Queen Against Richmond

Andrew Brent lived with his wife in the country, an hour's journey from London. They were a handsome couple, and lived in an attractive house which Sally Brent was always redecorating. Brent had been successful as a silk and liked to indulge his wife's fancies and, on occasions, his own. On the morning of Richmond's trial they breakfasted together as usual at 7.30 a.m. There was no silence rule at breakfast with the Brents. He reserved that for the train journey, during which he more or less successfully resisted all attempts at conversation while he read the paper.

'Darling,' said Sally. 'I think I'm going to have a grey and white Regency paper in the drawing-room.'

'Lovely,' said Brent.

'And I'm going to paint the upstairs bathroom green and gold.'

'Green and gold? What for?'

'Fun, darling. And I'm going to banish Aunt Louise's picture to the upstairs lavatory.'

'What's going to happen to my masterpiece?'

At one time Brent had dabbled in painting and one of his works, which had been exhibited at the South-East Wessex Art Society, price five guineas (unsold), had been thought by Sally to have sufficient merit to justify its being hung in their new house.

'It's being promoted,' she said, 'to the downstairs lavatory.'

'I shall get a swollen head,' he said. 'By the way,' he added, after a slight pause, 'this case today's a heavy one, and I may have to have a long conference after court.'

'Meaning?' said Sally.

'Meaning,' said Brent, 'that, as I've got one or two other conferences as well, I may have to take the late train back.'

'Dinner in town?' asked Sally.

'I'm afraid so. I'll try and make the early train, but I doubt if I can get it, and I'll give you a ring.'

'Thank you for telling me, darling,' said Sally. 'I think I'm going to change the paper in your study to something more exciting.'

'But why, darling?'

'I think you need a change, darling—you have such a drab existence—working all day in town—dinner all by yourself, and then that horrible last train which stops at nearly every station—and finally a drab, dull wife to find asleep when you come home. You need some uplift. Something new in the study. Short of a beautiful new secretary there's nothing like a change of paint or paper.'

'Whatever you say, darling,' said Brent. 'I *will* try and get back for dinner,' he added.

'Not for me,' said Sally. 'I'll go over and see Mother if you're not coming. I was just thinking of you, darling, in that horrid station restaurant. If you have got to stay up, why don't you go somewhere nice?'

Brent looked quickly at his wife. 'No point, really,' he muttered into his coffee.

Half an hour later he was in the train trying to read *The Times*.

'See you're prosecuting in that insurance case,' said one of the three other occupants of his carriage.

'Yes,' said Brent.

'A hundred thousand pounds is a lot of money,' said his assailant.

'Yes,' said Brent.

'Pretty good mugs to pay up one day and discover the fraud the next. He is guilty, I suppose?'

'That's what I shall invite the jury to say,' said Brent.

'You lawyers! Close as clams. Bet you tell your wife, though. Trust a woman to find out what you're really thinking. Don't you think so, old man?'

Brent did not answer.

'Eh? old man?'

'I dare say.'

'Don't you ever feel awkward when you prosecute an innocent man and have him sent to prison?'

'It's never happened to me.'

'D'you mean to say that an innocent person is never convicted?'

'I didn't say that. I said I've never prosecuted one.'

'Do you always get a conviction then?'

'Oh, no.'

'Then you mean they're guilty but they get off?'

'Precisely.'

'But if they're found not guilty, old man, you can't say they're guilty, can you?'

'No.'

'But you've just said so, old man. Not bad to score off a lawyer. Don't suppose that often happens to you.'

'We're not infallible, you know.'

'D'you make many mistakes, old man?'

'I hope not.

'But some?'

'Of course—who doesn't?'

'D'you ever defend people as well as prosecute?'

'Sometimes.'

'Pretty awful to defend an innocent man and have him found guilty and hanged.'

'No worse than for a doctor, who kills his patient by accident.'

'But d'you think that ever happens these days, old man—with penicillin and all those things?'

'There's always the human factor.'

'Then judges make mistakes too, old man?'

'They certainly do.'

'That's rather alarming, old man. Why do they become judges, then? Pretty awful not to be able to trust a judge to be right. That'd shake some people if they knew. I had a case once. Glad I didn't know the risk I was running. The judge said he believed every word I said. I should hope so too. I'd learned my evidence by heart. My wife had to hear me before breakfast. Like repetition at school. I can almost remember it now. Of course it was pretty nearly all true. There was just one bit which my lawyer said I should put another way round. Clever chaps, you lawyers. Not perjury, you know. Just a better way of saying the same thing. But you want to read the paper, old man. Don't mind me. Don't expect you get much time for reading.'

'No,' said Brent.

'Train's about the only place.'

'Yes.'

'Then some annoying beggar like me interrupts the whole time.'

Brent did not answer.

'Must make you want to chuck things at him, old man. Is there any news, by the way? I never see the paper till the evening. Nor will you today, old man, at this rate. You must think me a bore.'

He laughed cheerfully.

'Odd thing,' he went on, 'I don't mind being thought a bore. I am one, I know. Known it for a long time. Only thing to do is to make the best of it. I can just imagine what you'll be saying tonight, old man. There was a dreadful bore in my carriage this morning. Talked incessantly. Stopped me reading. There ought to be a notice in some carriages "No talking"—that's what you'll say, isn't it, old man?'

'With luck,' said Brent, 'I shall have forgotten the incident.'
He had had enough.

'Oh,' said the man. 'No need to take offence, old man,' and
relapsed into silence.

All this time there were converging on the Old Bailey—
where the trial was to take place—the various interested
parties. Miss Clinch had bought a new dress for the occasion,
and a new hat. She looked at herself in the glass with some
satisfaction.

'Rosamund,' she said, 'you're quite a clever girl. I wonder
what he'll get?'

She was not in the least malicious, but she loved to be
proved right, and this was, therefore, a very special occasion.
As everyone agreed, £100,000 is a lot of money. And it would
be entirely due to her that Richmond had been brought to
book. She bore no grudge against him at all. Crime was no
doubt his business, just as hers was claims-assessing. Indeed,
once he'd been convicted, she might even be sorry for him—
to have got so near to success and then to have been caught
when he must have thought himself quite safe. He had
reckoned without Rosamund Clinch. Mr Tewkesbury had
not progressed as far as Miss Clinch. He was asleep in his
bath. He would wake up as the water cooled off. A couple of
whiskies and he would be on his way, not more than half an
hour or so late. His client Mr Richmond had to be punctual,
indeed his appointment was timed for 10 o'clock—although
the trial was not due to begin until 10.30. Stanmore lived
in the Temple, and it only took him ten minutes to walk
from his chambers. He need not leave them till ten. Mr Justice
Short, who was to try the case, lived—like Brent—about an
hour's journey out of London. He was everything the English
public rightly think a judge should be. Quiet on the bench,
courteous, judicial, a sound lawyer, patient, with a controlled
sense of humour. He had only once surprised people. After
being a widower for twenty-six years, he had suddenly married
a beautiful girl thirty-five years younger than himself.

Moreover not only was she so much younger than himself, and so very good-looking, but she had been an actress and a model, and she liked gay friends and gay parties. The judge had never particularly cared for gay parties, except in his earliest youth. It was all something of a mystery, but it made excellent reading in the gossip columns of the newspapers and the judge, who had seldom seen his picture in the papers, now saw it far more often than he liked. Nor did he particularly care for such references as—'The judge is Mr Justice Short, who recently married the beautiful model Vivienne Colley.' However, there was nothing he could do about it, and it was certainly compensated for by the fact that he and his new young wife were extremely happy. At first after the marriage he had tried to please her by going out frequently at night, and making himself as agreeable as he could at gay parties. But it was not very long before he found the pace too hot and the interminable cabaret singers too boring and too late. In consequence Vivienne started to go out—with his entire approval—without him, and it became quite a usual thing for her picture to appear in one of the glossy periodicals at some night club. This gave the gossip writers some fun. For example: 'Here is the lovely Vivienne Short, enjoying a joke with her companion at the Soft Shoe Club. (Her husband is no doubt composing one of his reserved judgments. I wonder what his judgment would have been on the new cabaret turn Elise—the girl who appears in very little else)'. The judge did have to speak to his wife once about this sort of thing. He pointed out to her how important it was that she should do nothing which could bring either of them into disrepute. On that occasion she had been photographed dancing with a notorious co-respondent. She had explained that she'd no idea who he was at the time, and the judge explained to her how careful she must be. Vivienne had said she quite understood, and that she would be more careful in future.

On the way to Court the judge read the depositions, and was glad to see that Brent was prosecuting. They were old friends, but that was not the reason he was glad. The case was likely to take some time and it was a great help to have a prosecutor who was able and fair.

At half-past ten precisely the trial began. It had excited quite an amount of public interest. Since the House of Commons voted to abolish the death penalty murder had lost something of its glamour, while £100,000—even in some-one else's pocket—will always be glamorous. After the jury had been sworn and the accused had pleaded Not Guilty, Brent rose and began to open the case.

'May it please your Lordship, members of the jury, I appear in this case with my learned friend Mr Bellows for the prosecu-tion, and the accused is represented by my learned friend Mr Stanmore. As you have heard, members of the jury, the charge against the accused is that he obtained a hundred thousand pounds from the Positive Insurance Company Limited by false pretences with intent to defraud. First of all I will tell you the undisputed facts. On the 16th June last, the accused insured this sum of money against loss by burglary or housebreaking while at his house for a period of twenty-four hours. On the very next day he reported that it had been stolen. He said his house had been burgled and that he had been struck on the head and tied up by two men. The insurance company was not satisfied about the claim, and an action was eventually brought by the accused to recover what he said was the sum due under the policy. After the trial had progressed a little time, the defendants eventually withdrew their defence and agreed to pay the sum claimed. Had they known the true facts at the time they would not have paid one penny. But they did not know the true facts. Now, members of the jury, this is a somewhat unusual case. Let me say at once that I am not in a position to prove positively that the accused did not have a burglary, though you may very well form an opinion about that matter when you have heard the other facts which will be placed before you. Members of the jury, these are the other facts. When the accused effected this insurance, he said that his name was William Richmond, and that he had never previously made any claim against any insurance company. He repeated this statement when he was interviewed after the alleged burglary. As a matter of fact it is common ground that that statement was in fact untrue, but I want to make it quite plain at the outset that the particular untruth to which I am referring at the moment does not in any way form the basis of this prosecution.'

Brent then referred to the claim made twenty years previously in respect of the car accident, and went on:

'If that was the only untruth, the accused would not now be in the dock. I am prepared to accept that he had entirely forgotten about that trifling matter. But there are other matters which are very far from trifling—which he cannot have forgotten about.'

'I'm sorry to interrupt my learned friend,' said Stanmore, 'but he ought not to say that *my client* cannot have forgotten.'

'I shall be obliged if my learned friend will let me open the case in my own way,' said Brent.

'Not if it's unfair,' replied Stanmore.

'I think it would be better,' said the judge, 'if the jury heard you one at a time. These cases are sometimes difficult for the jury to follow even then. They are impossible if there are constant interruptions.'

'I hope my learned friend will be fair then, my Lord,' said Stanmore.

'If I'm not,' said Brent, 'I'm sure his Lordship will intervene.'

'With the utmost respect,' said Stanmore, 'his Lordship does not know all the facts.'

'Neither will the jury at this rate,' said the judge.

'I'm sorry, my Lord,' persisted Stanmore, 'but my learned friend is opening this case as though it were admitted that certain other claims, to which he is about to refer, were made by my client. In fact it is hotly disputed that any of these other claims were anything to do with my client.'

'Mr Stanmore,' said the judge, 'the jury has not yet heard

of these other claims. They cannot know what you are talking
about. Would it not be better if you reserved your intervention
for later—if necessary, and I suspect that you will then find
you do not need to make it.'

'If your Lordship pleases,' said Stanmore.

'Now, members of the jury,' continued Brent, 'I was telling
you that there were certain matters which, if you accept the
evidence for the prosecution, the accused cannot have forgotten. The case for the prosecution is simply this. Some years
ago a man named Cholmeley made a claim for loss of jewellery
on the Black & White Insurance Company. I shall plainly
be able to prove to you that it was a fraudulent claim—indeed,
I do not think that there will be any dispute about that. The
issue which you will mainly have to consider is the identity of
Mr Cholmeley. He was paid by the company who, at the time,
thought the claim was genuine. By the time they had discovered the fraud, Mr Cholmeley had disappeared. Not very
long afterwards, a man named Urquhart made a claim on
another company. That claim too was paid. That too was
found to be fraudulent. By the time of the discovery Mr
Urquhart also had disappeared. At about the same time a
Mr Smith had made a claim against yet a third company. No
doubt you have guessed what I am going to say. It was another
fraudulent claim, it was paid before the fraud was discovered
and, when it was discovered, Mr Smith was gone. Now,
members of the jury, it may not surprise you to learn that
these three gentlemen—if that is not too flattering a term to
apply to them—were not particularly anxious to be recognized
and in consequence each of them was only seen, as far as is
known, on one occasion by a representative of the insurance
company concerned. The rest of the transaction was conducted
by correspondence. In those circumstances you may again not
be surprised to learn that no one could positively identify
Mr Cholmeley, Mr Urquhart or Mr Smith, but there were
two things that can be said of them—each was lame and each
was bald. Members of the jury—so is the prisoner—lame and

bald. That is a remarkable coincidence, members of the jury, and in due course I am going to ask you to say that all these three men, Cholmeley, Urquhart and Smith are now in the dock—and I am not referring to the warders beside the prisoner. We say that the accused is Cholmeley, Urquhart and Smith. Now, members of the jury, I have already indicated to you that I am not in a position to call anyone who can in fact identify the prisoner as the same man who made these other insurances, and I expect you have already begun to wonder if the prosecution is going to ask you to say that, merely because of this extraordinary coincidence of baldness and lameness, all these four men are the man in the dock. Let me say at once, members of the jury, I am going to do nothing of the kind. Remarkable as the coincidence is, it would not be sufficient to justify a criminal charge. There is, however, a further coincidence, members of the jury, which it will be my submission to you clinches the matter. Cholmeley, Urquhart and Smith disappeared, but they did not disappear without trace. They left something behind them; they left behind them— they could not help doing so—the letters they had written to the various companies. Now let me say again at once that none of the signatures to these letters, the body of all of which was typed, can be proved to have been written by the same person. Those particular names contain very few letters in common. Was that why they were chosen? And no expert is prepared to say that the same hand wrote them all. They can only say that this is possible. But, members of the jury, this case does not rest on the evidence of hand-writing experts, who may not always be infallible. The letters I have told you were typed, and typewriters have their own idiosyncrasies—just as much as human beings . . . indeed, more so—and I am in a position to prove—not as a probability, but as a plain indisputable fact, that all the letters sent by Cholmeley, Urquhart and Smith were typed on one and the same machine, and that letters sent by the accused were also typed on that machine.'

Brent paused to let this sink into the minds of the jury.

'Members of the jury,' he went on after the pause, 'I am in a position to prove this fact to you as conclusively as it is possible to prove anything, and indeed I think you will find that my learned friend, whose clients have, of course, been given every opportunity to test the matter, will not dispute it.'

'That is perfectly correct,' intervened Stanmore. 'We are satisfied that all these letters were written on the same type-writer.'

'I am obliged to my friend,' said Brent, 'and you, members of the jury, may in the circumstances be excused for wondering what possible defence there can now be to the charge. Let me remind you that the charge is simply that the accused induced the insurance company to insure him and to pay this claim by falsely pretending that he had never made a previous claim on any insurance company, and that in doing so he intended to defraud. When I started to open this case, I said that there were facts—unlike the trifling matter of the car insurance claim —which the accused could not have forgotten. And if you are satisfied that he was in fact Cholmeley, Urquhart and Smith, I doubt if it will take you very long to come to the conclusion that the prosecution's case has been made out beyond any possibility of doubt. But there is a further matter about which I have to tell you, members of the jury—one which puts the coincidence of the baldness and lameness very much into the shade. Before the accused was prosecuted, it was thought desirable to give him an opportunity to explain about the letters, and a Miss Clinch accompanied by an officer from Scotland Yard called on him for the purpose. The accused stoutly denied that he was Cholmeley, Urquhart or Smith, or that he had ever heard of any of them or had anything to do with them or their claims. It was then pointed out to him that the typewriter used in each case was the same; he was asked where he had obtained it. After a little hesitation he said that he had bought it from a barrow boy only very recently. Well, members of the jury, you might perhaps hesitate to buy a typewriter that had to be extracted from among the bananas and oranges . . .'

Stanmore got up.

'I can't stop my friend from trying to be funny,' he said, 'but he can at least be accurate. This was not a fruit barrow—it was old clothes and the like.'

'I'm sorry,' said Brent. 'I should have said from among the pants and vests. You may think it an odd way to buy a typewriter, but, if it is true, just consider what it involves. It means that by pure coincidence the lame and bald Messrs Cholmeley, Urquhart and Smith happened to dispose of their typewriter and that it happened to find its way into the hands of the lame and bald Mr Richmond. I don't know how many typewriters there are in the country, but the chances of any particular second-hand typewriter falling into a person's hands are many hundred thousand to one—probably many million to one. Think of the coincidences necessary to enable it to happen. But this particular coincidence—or perhaps alleged coincidence is a more suitable phrase—this alleged coincidence beats everything. It required that the way in which and time at which the typewriter was disposed of by Cholmeley, Urquhart and Smith —and the way in which the alleged barrow boy dealt with his own affairs, should so take place that the lame and bald prisoner should happen to meet the barrow boy and buy the typewriter from him. Strange things do happen in the world— many strange things, but can you conceive, members of the jury, coincidences such as those which the defence in this case rests on? Just imagine, members of the jury, the accused had to get up at such a time, go out at such a time, go by a particular route, so that—in spite of his lameness, I say nothing of his baldness—he should happen to meet the barrow boy. You see, members of the jury, if the accused had said he bought it from a reputable dealer, the history of the machine could have been traced. He has to say he bought it from a source which can't be traced, so that we shall never know how a valuable machine like a typewriter came to be in the hands of

a barrow boy. We shall never know from whom he got it.
Really, members of the jury, if this were not a criminal charge,
in which it is necessary for the prosecution to prove its case
beyond all reasonable doubt, I should not have taken up so
much of your time in opening. I shall have to call a considerable body of evidence to prove the facts I have outlined to
you, but if the evidence is as I have stated I venture to suggest
to you, members of the jury, that you have never in fact or
fiction come across a more impudent defence than that raised
by the accused. You see—once he admits that the typewriter
has been his for several years, the game is up. He has to say
he has only bought it recently. So he invites you to believe a
series of coincidences which, I suggest to you, cannot take
place in human affairs. It has been said that, if a million
monkeys who could type typed blindly for a number of million
years, eventually the works of Shakespeare would be produced.
Don't you think, members of the jury, that is more likely than
the explanation relied on by the accused? I shall now, with
the help of my learned junior, call the evidence.'

The witnesses on the first day of the trial were the various
people who were concerned with the previous claims. They
were all asked if they could identify the accused as the man
whom they had seen, and they each replied that they could
not. But they were equally certain that the man they *had*
seen was lame and bald, and a man of similar build to that
of the prisoner. At the end of the day Stanmore had a
conference with Mr Tewkesbury and their client at his
chambers.

'What do you consider my chances are?' Richmond asked
Stanmore.

'Not very large, I'm afraid.'

'But I'm innocent—absolutely innocent—I assure you.'

'That may be,' said Stanmore, 'but put yourself in the
position of the jury. Look at the coincidences which must have
happened if you are innocent. Who can you expect to believe
them?'

At that moment Mr Tewkesbury, who had appeared to be sleeping peacefully, opened his eyes and said:

'I believe them, my dear sir, I believe them profoundly,' and closed his eyes again.

'That means then,' said Mr Richmond to Stanmore, ignoring his solicitor's support, 'that *you* don't believe me.'

'It's of no importance what I believe. I'm here to put forward your case as best I can. I'm not trying you. That's for the judge and jury.'

'But if you believed in me wouldn't it make your task easier?'

'Not in the least,' said Stanmore. 'I've long ago given up considering whether to believe my clients or not. Now, if the judge believed you—that would be another matter.'

'You don't think he does?'

'He hasn't heard you yet—but your difficulty is the million to one chance—or the many million to one chance on which your case rests.'

'Coincidences do happen, Mr Stanmore, very strange ones indeed, and this is one of them. I do assure you that I am absolutely innocent. It's terrible not to be believed. That's why innocent people have been convicted in the past—because no one would believe them. Surely you can do something to make them believe a true case.'

'I will do all I can.'

'Suppose we found the man who sold it to me? Would that help?'

'Well—of course it would, but Mr Tewkesbury has advertised in the press for him and he hasn't come forward.'

'That doesn't mean that he doesn't exist.'

'Of course it doesn't, but it does mean you can't prove that he does exist.'

'I've scoured the streets for him. I'll try again. But I suppose if I found him by a lucky chance you'd say that it was another coincidence.'

'Provided it really was the man, that wouldn't matter.'

Mr Richmond hesitated for a moment and then said:

'There's something quite different I want to ask you about. As I was coming away from the court, I thought I saw a car with the judge and counsel for the prosecution inside with him. I may have been wrong, as I haven't seen the judge without his wig, but that's what it looked like to me.'

'I dare say you did see them. They're very old friends.'

'That seems a bit hard on me—the judge and the prosecution being buddies.'

'I can assure you,' said Stanmore, 'that it doesn't make the slightest difference to you. Judges have lots of friends at the Bar and they know most of the experienced practitioners quite well. They couldn't appear in cases at all if knowing a judge were a disqualification.'

'But they're close friends, you say?'

'Yes—but what of it? I know Brent quite well, although I'm not a close friend of his. But if the judge were my brother and Brent my brother-in-law it wouldn't make a ha'porth of difference as to how this trial's conducted. One thing you can be certain of—they won't discuss this case at all while they're together.'

'D'you mean that? It must be a temptation.'

'Not in the least. They're used to it.'

'Oh—well, I suppose you know best, and I suppose it's all right. It's a bit shattering at first though. Hope you don't mind my mentioning it.'

'Not a bit. I quite understand your feelings, though that is one thing I can guarantee you're all right about. Now, about this barrow boy—there's no harm in your trying again. They often go on the same beats, I believe.'

'If I find him, will you believe me?'

'I repeat that it doesn't matter what I believe.'

'I dare say—but will you?'

'How can I tell without seeing the man?'

'You mean I might produce him out of a hat. Pretty dangerous that sort of thing.'

'Very—but it does happen.'

'You think I'm guilty as well, don't you?' said Mr Richmond. 'You don't believe my house was ever burgled, that I was ever tied up or knocked on the head, do you?'

'Well, no one can prove you weren't. The prosecution have admitted that.'

'But it doesn't seem to make any difference. I can be struck on the head and tied up *and* lose a hundred thousand pounds, but—because of a ruddy typewriter—I'm guilty of fraud. Has it ever occurred to you what an incredible idiot I am if it *was* me who used the same typewriter?'

Mr Tewkesbury opened his eyes.

'It has indeed,' he said, and closed them again.

'Mr Richmond,' said Stanmore, 'of course I'll use that argument for all I'm worth, and there's a lot in it. Would a man who was out for such a big prize be stupid enough to make a mistake like that? Oh, yes—I'll ram that one home. But the trouble is—and please don't think I'm being offensive in saying this—I'm only telling you what the prosecution will say—the trouble is that it is a fact that even the most astute criminals sometimes make very silly mistakes, even sillier than that.'

'Well, I wish I could convince you that you are defending an absolutely innocent man. It's terrible feeling you're disbelieved. It's like being shut up in a place. It's awful. The truth must come out—surely it must. Is there anything I can say or do at least to make you believe in me?'

'You make the judge and prosecuting counsel believe you when you give your evidence.'

'Prosecuting counsel! That's asking too much. He's paid to disbelieve me.'

'Not a bit of it. If you convinced him you might be innocent, he'd make a very different speech to the jury from the one he's just made. It isn't his job to get you convicted at all costs—only to see the case for the prosecution is fairly put.'

'Well—he didn't seem to have much doubt about it this morning when he opened the case.'

'That's true,' said Stanmore, 'and that's why I say it's really up to you—when you give your evidence. But it's the jury you've got to convince . . . though, of course, a helping hand from the judge would be pretty certain to get you off.'

'But I won't get that at the moment?'

'Nothing in the world is certain, but at the moment I should be very surprised if you did.'

'You still don't believe I was burgled, do you? You think I knocked myself on the head, don't you?'

'Mr Richmond,' said Stanmore, 'we've been over this before. If a barrister had to believe his client before he could defend him—precious few prisoners would be defended at all, at any rate not by very intelligent counsel. I can only tell you that I'll do my best to get you off and if, because I'm not prepared to say to you that I believe your story implicitly, you'd like to consult someone else, by all means do so.'

'Oh—no,' said Richmond. 'I'm very happy to have you appearing for me, but I don't seem to have much chance of convincing the judge and jury if I can't convince my own counsel.'

'We must hope for the best,' said Stanmore—and with that his client had to be contented. They woke Mr Tewkesbury up and, on waking, he expressed the view that the case was going very nicely—very nicely indeed.

'Believe me, Mr Stanmore,' he said, 'though I'm only a very humble solicitor there's little I don't know about the inside of the Old Bailey. Many's the client for whom I've snatched a victory out of what looked like certain defeat. I remember once, before Mr Justice——'

But Richmond interrupted.

'I've an appointment I'm afraid,' he said, 'you tell me on the way. Good afternoon, Mr Stanmore, and thank you for all your help and tolerance.'

He took Mr Tewkesbury by the arm and led him firmly out of Stanmore's room. As he went out Mr Tewkesbury said:

'Good-bye, my dear sir, we shall meet at Philippi. Meanwhile, to the Cock. Lay on, Macduff; and damn'd be him who first cries: "Hold—enough." '

CHAPTER NINE

Domestic Coincidences

BRENT did after all catch the late train home. He did not appear to be detained so much by late conferences as by—among other things—a telephone call, and a drink at their club with Mr Justice Short.

'This is the best hour in the day,' said the judge—'for me, that is. You, poor fellow, have to go and work. Still you look very well on it.'

'I survive,' said Brent, 'but it's nice to think the week-end is near. Incidentally, when are you and Vivienne going to dine with us? It's years since you last did.'

'I'd enjoy it,' said the judge, 'if Vivienne isn't too full up with her parties. I believe your Sally sees more of her than I do.'

'They do see a lot of each other, don't they—make what I would call a formidable shopping combination.'

Half an hour later the judge left for his home, while Brent kept an appointment. Richmond meanwhile was going through the streets of London, looking carefully at every barrow boy he met. Miss Clinch went to the pictures, while Mr Tewkesbury held forth in the private bar of a public house.

'Mark my words, my dear sir,' he said to a complete stranger—with whom he was exchanging the normal alcoholic confidences—'mark my words, the day will come when the law will be one vast slot machine.'

'Meaning?' queried his companion.

'Automatic judges, my dear sir. No barristers or solicitors. You just put down your statement of the case, the other side puts down his, push 'em in the machine—pull the lever and, after a few minutes' calculation, the answer comes out on a ticket. No long arguments, no lawyer's fees, all done by the State. Put in your guinea and out comes your judgment. Not in six months—but in six minutes. Magna Carta at last. Justice delayed is justice denied, my dear sir.'

'But what use will you solicitors be? Your living will be gone.'

'Ah,' said Mr Tewkesbury, placing his finger alongside his nose. 'Ah! That's a secret. But I'll tell you. I shall invent the machine.'

'Remarkable.'

'You may indeed say so, sir. And perhaps one could make a little on the side, too, if you follow me. An extra guinea or so might make the machine move to one side or the other. As a matter of fact,' he said, in a confidential voice, 'I shall be inside writing the judgments. No reasons given, mind you. That's what spoils the judgments of today. Who wants pages of reasons? What people want is the decision. And quickly. Judgment for the Plaintiff, or judgment for the Defendant. Divorces just the same. But I'll have to keep up a pretty high speed with them, or there'll be no improvement on the present system.'

By the time Mr Tewkesbury was ready, able and willing to go to sleep on the pavement again, the judge had arrived home, but he was not his usual genial self when Vivienne greeted him with a kiss. He had seen something in the paper on the way home which he found most disquieting. She seemed at first not to sense this.

'They've just been mentioning your case on the wireless,' she said, shortly after he'd come in. 'A hundred thousand pounds is an awful lot of money. What'll he get, darling?'

'He isn't convicted yet,' said the judge gruffly.

'Don't be pompous, darling. It's me you're talking to. What'll he get?'

'I tell you—it's for the jury to convict, not me.'

'But you give them a hand sometimes, don't you, darling?'

'Well, if I do, I shouldn't, and that's all there is to it.'

'You sound cross. What is it?'

The judge did not reply.

'Is it me? Have I done something awful?' she went on. 'I can't think what.'

'You can't think what,' he repeated, almost as grimly as when he addressed a really experienced criminal.

'Oh, dear, it must be something terribly bad. Is this where I get sent to bed?'

'You must be serious. It is serious. You know perfectly well what it is.'

'I don't,' said Vivienne, 'really, darling, I don't.'

He handed her a newspaper.

'I suppose you know nothing about that,' he said in his Old Bailey voice.

She looked at a picture in the newspaper for a short time. Then she scrutinized it more closely.

'Good Lord,' she said at last, 'how extraordinary.'

'It's not extraordinary at all,' he said, now well into his Old Bailey stride. 'Three months ago you promised me that it would not happen again. You must realize my position. You know I want you to have a good time. It's only fair you should. But if I've told you once I've told you a hundred times, you mustn't do anything to make people talk about you— unpleasantly, I mean. You can't help your picture being in the paper. But you can help it being next to that.'

The photograph showed Vivienne sitting arm in arm at a night club with a man of about forty. He was in fact a well-known West End gambler, who had been through the Divorce Court at least three times.

'That man's notorious,' he went on, 'he may even have been up in front of me. It really is too bad. Can't I trust you at all?'

'May the prisoner speak?' asked Vivienne.

'Well—what is there to say?'

'I thought everyone was innocent until they're proved guilty.

You've convicted me without a hearing and are waiting to pass sentence before I've said a word. Is that British justice? Why, I'm not sure it wouldn't give me good grounds for appeal. Even you let the prisoner or his counsel address the jury—even if it is a formality, as you're going to tell them they've jolly well got to convict.'

'Well, what d'you want to say?'

'Quite simple, my Lord, it wasn't me.'

'What d'you mean, it wasn't you?'

'What I say. It wasn't me. This'—and she pointed to the picture of the woman—'isn't me.'

The judge looked at it closely.

'But it is you,' he said after a moment. 'It's exactly like.'

'Yes,' she said, 'that's what's so extraordinary. It *is* exactly like.'

'I can't believe it,' he said. 'And look,' he added, 'you've got that dress on.'

She looked at the picture again.

'That's odder than ever,' she said.

'You're not really saying it isn't you,' he went on.

'But I am, darling. Didn't you hear me?'

'But you don't mean it?'

'Of course I mean it.'

The judge picked up the paper and then threw it on a chair.

'Look, Vivienne,' he said, 'this man I'm trying today—he's got a cock and bull story about having bought a typewriter from a barrow boy—a story which no one in their senses would believe. But he's a crook—he's in the dock . . . I don't expect you to behave like one of those.'

'I thought he hadn't been convicted yet,' said Vivienne. 'You wouldn't even tell me what he's going to get. Now you say he's a crook. I can see what I'm in for. Find me guilty without giving me a chance. All the same, it wasn't me. It's just somebody very like me.'

'Very, very like you.'

'Yes, very—very like me, but not me.'

She picked up the paper again.

'And look,' she said, 'I haven't a necklace like that.'

'Haven't you? It's just like the one your mother gave you.'

'But these are much bigger, darling—can't you see? These couldn't possibly be real. Mother's were.'

'Well, I can't help it,' he said. 'I know my own wife's face. That's you.'

'But you don't darling. It isn't me. I promise.'

'Well—where were you then?'

'I was with Charles and Mary. We went to a lot of places—but——' she stopped, and looked at the letterpress—'not the Bulgaria. And look, it doesn't say it was me. "Mr Brink and a friend enjoying a laugh." They wouldn't have left my name out, now, would they? Much too good for business. And with you at the Old Bailey this week trying that cock and bull barrow boy story case.'

That's certainly a point, thought the judge. But it's Vivienne's photograph—it must be.

'Well, it's quite simple,' she said after a moment, 'ring up Charles and ask him.'

'I'm not going to start doing that.'

She pressed home her advantage.

'Well, just make an excuse to ask them something, and bring me into the conversation. A lawyer should have no difficulty in doing that.'

'No,' he said, 'I can't believe you . . . but I'm not going to check up on you with friends.'

'Well, you must believe me, darling,' she said. 'I really am telling the truth this time. Really and truly. I know I haven't always. But it is really this time. And I do love you—and I won't ever let you down again.'

'Again?'

'You are a judge, aren't you. I meant after last time.'

'I thought you meant this time.'

'There isn't a this time. It's just an extraordinary coincidence. I wonder who she is.'

'Mrs Cholmeley or Mrs Urquhart or Mrs Smith, I expect,' said the judge.

'Who are they?'

'Never mind,' said the judge. 'Let's have a drink and forget it.'

'That's better. Probation?'

'You haven't been convicted.'

'It was a near thing.'

'It's these coincidences we don't like,' said the judge. 'They do happen in real life, of course, but almost never when they'd be of any use to anyone. It's only criminals and crooks who rely on them for the most part.'

'And judge's wives,' said Vivienne.

'Well, let's hope there aren't any more. But I suppose, if you've a real double, there may be.'

It was some considerable time after the judge and his wife had agreed to forget the matter of the photograph that Brent arrived home. Sally was in bed. Some hours before he had arrived, an acquaintance of hers had telephoned and, after discussing various unimportant matters which she asserted were the reason for her call, mentioned almost casually that she had just seen Andrew dining in a restaurant with a good-looking blonde girl.

'I didn't know Andrew had a sister,' she had said.

'He hasn't.'

'Oh—I didn't know you had one.'

'I haven't.'

'I see. Well . . . I do hope I haven't said anything out of turn. I wouldn't have dreamed of mentioning it if I'd thought . . .'

'Thought what?' asked Sally sharply. 'Of course I knew he was dining with a friend of ours.'

'I didn't catch the name.'

'Mind your own bloody business,' Sally had said, and regretted it immediately afterwards. But she was not pleased —as Andrew discovered as soon as he arrived. However he was not a barrister for nothing.

'Sorry I'm late, darling,' he said. 'But a funny thing . . . who d'you think I happened to run into?'

'I've no idea.'

'Polly Turner that was.'

'What—the girl you nearly married?'

'Yes—wasn't it extraordinary?'

'Most.'

'I was just coming along from the Temple, wondering where to have a bite, when I just happened to run into her.'

'Has she changed?'

'No, not really.'

'Still pretty as a picture?'

'Oh—not bad, you know,' Andrew said a little uncomfortably.

'Well . . . it's nice of you to have told me.'

'What do you mean?' he said, with a presentable show of injured innocence.

'What I say. I shouldn't have known anything about it if you hadn't, should I?' A sudden thought struck her.

'Unless, of course, you happened to see Sybil Saunders there.'

'Sybil? No, I didn't see her.'

'Well, she saw you. So you were very wise to have told me.'

'Don't be perfectly ridiculous. I'd have told you anyway. Hang it—I did tell you.'

'The truth, the whole truth and nothing but the truth?'

'Yes, of course.'

'Something of a coincidence, wasn't it?'

'Yes, it was.'

'And not the first. If my recollection is right, three months ago you happened to meet her in a tube and you dined with her afterwards.'

'Well, what of it?'

'You don't really ask me to believe it's happened again? There are about I don't know how many million women in London—the chances of your meeting her—that one particular woman—are about how many to one, would you say?'

'Well, I did.'

'I don't doubt you met her. But not by chance—not twice in three months by chance. I can hear you addressing a jury on the subject: "Can you really believe, members of the jury . . ." '

'Oh—shut up,' said Andrew crossly.

'If only you'd tell me the truth,' said Sally, 'I shouldn't mind half so much—indeed I mightn't mind at all. But pretending about it makes it so much worse . . . and it might make me imagine things. Why should you lie to me if there was nothing you didn't want to hide?'

'I haven't lied to you. It was just a coincidence. How many more times have I got to say so? Why don't you believe me?'

'It must be dreadful,' said Sally, 'to tell the truth and not to be believed.'

'It is.'

'You look remarkably well on it.'

'You must believe me, darling. I really am telling the truth.' Andrew looked very earnest as he said this.

'Oh, well,' she said, 'I suppose I shall have to believe you—though I don't really. And you will see, won't you, there aren't any more coincidences?'

The next morning Mr Tewkesbury was absent from Court for the first hour. He was again in the dock at Bow Street.

'This is really outrageous,' said the magistrate, after he had found him guilty. 'Don't you ever realize that you're a solicitor?'

'Indeed I do, sir, indeed I do,' said Mr Tewkesbury. 'And are solicitors to be less privileged than their other more fortunate brethren?'

'You're not entitled to lie down in the street—nor is anyone else. If you must drink, why don't you do so decently at home?'

'I'll bear in mind the suggestion, sir,' said Mr Tewkesbury. '*Experto credo*, if I may coin a phrase.'

'Don't be impudent. I've a good mind to require you to find sureties for your good behaviour.'

'They would be forthcoming, sir,' said Mr Tewkesbury

affably. 'Indeed, in case they should be required I've brought
them with me. Call Mr Coggs and Mr Bloggs,' he said
authoritatively to the gaoler—who looked enquiringly at the
magistrate.

'Today you are fined twenty shillings.'

'What, no sureties?' complained Mr Tewkesbury. 'Can I
have Mr Coggs' and Mr Bloggs' expenses of coming here?'

'Take him away,' said the magistrate.

'*Au revoir*, sir, if not good-bye,' said Mr Tewkesbury, as they
hustled him out of the dock and through the door, to pay
his fine.

CHAPTER TEN

An Unexpected Witness

IT was some days afterwards that the case for the prosecution closed and Mr Richmond went into the witness box. In answer to Stanmore, he gave a short account of his life, stoutly denied that he was Cholmeley, Urquhart or Smith, and told his story about the burglary and his loss of £100,000. Brent then rose to cross-examine.

'Mr Richmond,' he asked in his first question, 'have you ever had a hundred thousand pounds in your possession in notes before?'

'No, sir. I have had large sums—such as twenty or thirty thousand but not, I think, more.'

'It is very unfortunate is it not,' said Brent, 'that this large sum should be stolen from you on the only occasion you have had such a large amount in your possession?'

'Most unfortunate.'

'For the insurance company,' commented Brent.

'Not for them only,' said Mr Richmond. 'If I hadn't been robbed I shouldn't be here. It seems rather hard on a man to be charged with fraud just because he's had a burglary.'

'Don't make statements, just answer questions,' said the judge.

'You are lame, are you not?' was the next question.

'Unfortunately again—yes.'

'And bald?'

'You can see that for yourself, if I may say so.'

'You have heard the evidence of those other insurances, have you not?'

'I have.'

'Do you doubt any of it?'

'No, I can't say that I do.'

'It is somewhat remarkable, is it not, that you should all be lame and bald?'

'It is odd,' agreed Mr Richmond.

'And how would you describe the circumstances that you all used the same typewriter?'

'Very odd.'

'It is a very strange way of buying a typewriter, to buy it from a barrow boy.'

'It is indeed. I've never done such a thing before and I shall certainly never do it again.'

'If your story is true, don't you think it the most extra-ordinary thing that has ever happened to anyone in his life? That—lame and bald as you are—you should buy a typewriter which had been used by three lame and bald men or—if you like—by one lame and bald man who used three names in the process of his fraudulent practices?'

'It is certainly the most unpleasant thing that has ever happened to me.'

'If, of course, you'd bought the typewriter in the normal way, its antecedents might be traced.'

Mr Richmond said nothing.

'Well?' said Brent.

'What is the question?' asked Mr Richmond.

'Very difficult to find a particular barrow boy,' went on Brent, 'very easy to find a particular shop.'

'Both can be done,' said Mr Richmond.

'Everything is possible,' said Brent, 'but you haven't, I suppose, managed to find the barrow boy?'

'Well, as a matter of fact, I have,' said Mr Richmond.

'You say you have found him?' asked the judge.

'I'm afraid so,' said Mr Richmond.

'Why afraid?' asked the judge.

'Because it was another coincidence. And Mr Brent doesn't like coincidences, nor, I fear, does your Lordship.'

'Don't make speeches, or be impertinent please. Where did you find him?' asked the judge.

'Well, I apologize, my Lord, but I found him on the way to Court this morning.'

The sensation went round the whole Court. Apparently the spectators didn't think much of coincidences either.

'I really am sorry,' went on Mr Richmond apologetically. 'I've been looking for him for weeks, and I have to go and find him today. It's too bad.'

'Don't try to be funny,' said the judge.

'My Lord,' intervened Stanmore, 'I'm sure my client does not intend to be disrespectful. But your Lordship will remember the scorn which has been poured on my client's defence by my learned friend. Your Lordship may perhaps think that this has not passed altogether unnoticed by my client, and that he has, not perhaps unnaturally, become a little touchy on the subject.'

'Your client knows perfectly well how to behave,' said the judge. 'He must do so in the future.'

'I do apologize,' said Mr Richmond.

'Be quiet,' said the judge.

'Really, my Lord,' said Stanmore, 'if my client isn't to be allowed to apologize to your Lordship——'

'You be quiet too,' said the judge.

Miss Clinch, sitting next to Mr Waite, whispered to him:

'This ought to get him an extra year. It's called subornation of perjury. I looked it up.'

'He's not convicted yet,' said Mr Waite. 'He's a fly customer, if you ask me.'

'I don't see anything fly about him. The jury are laughing at him. I don't blame them. But I wonder what story they're going to tell? Where will he say he got the typewriter from?'

'So you happened to meet,' began Brent sarcastically, and

then, realizing that it might be better to treat it more seriously until he knew what the facts were, he changed it to: 'So this morning you met the barrow boy?'

'That is so.'

'Where?'

'In the Strand.'

'What is his name?'

'Brown.'

'Any Christian names?'

'I expect so, but I don't know them. I can't vouch for his name being Brown, either, but he said it was.'

'And where is he now?'

'Outside the Court.'

'Did he come voluntarily, or did you issue a subpœna?'

'He said he didn't mind coming.'

'You had no difficulty in recognizing him?'

'Well—I wasn't absolutely sure at first, but he looked like the man and, when I asked him, he remembered the type-writer.'

'Did you ask him where he got it from?'

'No,' answered Mr Richmond, 'I didn't. I thought I oughtn't to ask him questions as he was going to be a witness—except to make sure he was the man. I couldn't find my solicitor to tell him about it when I got to the Court.'

'So your counsel doesn't know about it?'

'Not till now. I had to surrender to my bail and he didn't come into court until just before ten-thirty. I'd got the man here, so I didn't think it mattered.'

'When you bought the typewriter, as you say, from Mr Brown, did you ask him where he'd got it?'

'I don't think so. It was a pretty decrepit-looking thing.'

'Weren't you afraid it might have been stolen?'

'I don't see why. If it had been brand new, or nearly new, it would have been a different matter. But it was an old machine—the sort of thing anyone might have got rid of for five or ten pounds.'

D

'The sort of machine a bald and lame man might want to get rid of, you mean?'

Stanmore got up.

'That's the sort of thing I meant, my Lord. Is it a fair way to ask a question? Full of comment and prejudice.'

'I apologize,' said Brent. 'My friend is quite right. Tell me, Mr Richmond,' he went on, 'how much do you say you paid for it?'

'I think it was ten pounds. It might have been twelve pounds.'

'Did you get a receipt?'

'Certainly not.'

'Have you seen a typewriter for sale in the streets before?'

'I can't say that I have, but I haven't really noticed all the things that are on all the barrows in the streets. I suspect you'd find a variety of objects if you really went into the matter.'

'Now I want to ask you about something else,' said Brent. 'You say you've never used the name of Cholmeley?'

'Never.'

'Nor Urquhart?'

'No. Nor Smith.'

'But you agree that the letters written by those three gentlemen were typed on this machine?'

'I am told so and I accept it.'

'It would be beyond the bounds of possibility, don't you agree, for there to have been three different men, all lame and bald, who each used this identical typewriter?'

'Isn't my friend making a speech in the guise of a question?' intervened Stanmore. 'How can my client answer that question better than anyone else? It's pure conjecture.'

'If you object, I won't press it,' said Brent.

'I don't mind answering the question,' said Richmond. 'In fact I should like to do so. Of course it is in the highest degree improbable that there were three men, and personally I don't believe there were; but incredible things happen in human affairs. When they happen, as they do, in everyday matters no

one doubts that they have happened. They just say—"how
extraordinary." But when it's a man in the dock who says it,
then everyone . . . well, I hope not everyone,' he said, turning
towards the jury, 'but some people,' and he turned towards
Brent, 'won't listen to them—won't even consider the possibility of their having happened. I'm being tried because I'm
the victim of two coincidences—only two mark you—that a
lame and bald man has cheated insurance companies and sold
his old typewriter. I am absolutely innocent, but you doubt
me,' and he turned towards Brent, with half a glance at the
judge, 'because you don't like coincidences.'

'Yes?' said Brent, after a pause. 'Anything else?'

'Ask him questions, Mr Brent, please,' said the judge, 'don't
invite him to make speeches. Mr Stanmore will do that most
adequately.'

Eventually Mr Richmond's cross-examination was completed, and Stanmore decided to call the barrow boy as his
next witness. He considered whether to ask Mr Tewkesbury
to obtain a proof from him first, but decided that it would be
more likely to do harm than good. If the man were telling the
truth he'd stand up to cross-examination. He gave his name as
William Brown. It was obvious that he intended to enjoy
every minute of his stay in the witness box. Quite evidently
he was one of those witnesses who love the public eye, and
that he intended to make the most of the limelight which was
temporarily shining on him. The very way in which he had
walked into the witness box proclaimed it. After taking the
oath, he had looked towards counsel's row and along it, very
much as a bully in a public house challenges all comers to
fight.

'What are you, Mr Brown?' asked Stanmore.

'What am I? A man, same as anyone else.'

'Behave yourself,' said the judge. 'What do you do for a
living?'

'Ah—that's different, my Lord. Anything most like.'

'Do you know the accused?'

'Oos 'e?'

'The man in the dock.'

'Oh.'

The witness looked at Mr Richmond.

'I seen 'im.'

'When?'

'S'arternoon.'

'It's only the morning now.'

'That's it, guv'nor. A hour ago like.'

'Had you seen him before?'

' 'E said so.'

'What do you mean "he said so?" '

' 'E said so.'

'When?'

'S'arternoon.'

'You mean an hour ago?'

'S'right.'

'Will you try to forget what he said to you, and tell me——'

'Forget what 'e said to me? 'Ere wot is this?'

'Apart from what the accused said to you,' said the judge, 'do you personally think you've seen him before?'

'What, s'arternoon?'

'Before this afternoon?'

'S'morning, then?'

'No,' said the judge, 'before this morning.'

' 'Ave I seen 'im before this morning?'

'Yes.'

' 'E said so.'

'I dare say he did,' said the judge, 'but was it true?'

'Ask 'im,' said the witness.

'Yes, Mr Stanmore?' said the judge, who felt the moment had come to retire from the arena.

'Have you ever had any business dealings with the accused?' asked Stanmore.

'Wot are they?'

'You have a barrow, haven't you?'

'Well, wot's wrong with that?'

'Nothing's wrong with that,' said Stanmore patiently.

'Well, that's all right. Can I go now?' said the witness.

'What do you sell on your barrow?' said Stanmore doggedly.

'Anything most like.'

'Have you ever sold anything to the accused?'

'Wot—'im?'

'Yes.'

' 'E said so.'

'Never mind what he said. Have you ever sold anything to him?'

' 'Ow should I know? Can't remember all my customers.'

Stanmore hesitated a moment before asking his next question. He had to bring this extremely difficult witness to the matter of the typewriter without putting the words into his mouth. It was no easy task.

'What goods do you usually sell?' he asked eventually.

'Anything most like.'

'Please give some examples.'

'Wotchermean?'

'Tell me some of the things you have sold.'

'To 'oom?'

'To anyone.'

'I ain't sold no one a pup.'

'I dare say you haven't. I want to know what you have sold.'

'Business isn't so good.'

'Perhaps not, but you sell something.'

' 'Course I do—got ter live.'

'Exactly,' persisted Stanmore. 'What do you sell in order to live?'

'I told you—anything most like.'

'Anything's nothing,' said Stanmore crossly.

'Oh, no, it ain't mister. Anything's something, ain't it, my Lord?'

'Counsel wants to know something that you have sold,' said the judge.

'Why does 'e want to know? There ain't nothing wrong in it.'

'No one says there's anything wrong. You just answer the question.'

'But if there ain't nothing wrong, what do they want to bring me 'ere for? I ain't used to these places.'

'Now pull yourself together and answer the question,' said the judge. 'Tell me something you sold last week.'

'Last week?'

'Yes.'

' 'Ad a 'oliday last week, my Lord.'

'All right—the week before.'

'Something I sold the week before?'

'Yes.'

' 'Ave ter think.'

'All right, think.'

The witness remained silent and scratched his head. After a minute or two the judge said:

'Well—what's the answer?'

'It was a bad week, my Lord, the week before. 'Ardly made anything.'

'Never mind about that. What did you sell?'

'Well,' said the witness, 'I did sell . . . but it wasn't mine, I was selling it for a friend—does that count?'

'What was it you were selling for a friend?'

'A pianer, my Lord.'

'But you hadn't a piano on your barrow?'

'Not likely—it was at 'ome, but I didn't actually sell it you know, not to sell it proper like.'

'Mr Stanmore,' said the judge, 'this is your witness. You'd better try to bring him to the point.'

'I'll try, my Lord. Tell me, Mr Brown, I suppose you sell rags?'

'Don't lead please,' said Brent.

'Well, there can't be any dispute about this,' said Stanmore.

'I dare say,' said Brent, 'but I know what happens later. I'll be obliged if you won't.'

'What do you sell?' repeated Stanmore.

'Anything I can lay me 'ands on honest.'

'But you don't remember selling anything to this gentleman?' asked Stanmore, pointing to Mr Richmond.

'I might 'ave.'

'Of course you might have—but did you?'

'It's no use telling me 'is name cos I wouldn't 'ave arst 'im,' volunteered the witness.

'It's no use telling you anything,' said Stanmore under his breath. 'Have you ever sold anyone a typewriter?' he said to the witness.

'Now, really,' said Brent.

'I'm perfectly entitled to ask him that question generally,' said Stanmore.

'Well, you've asked it anyway,' said the judge. 'What's the answer? Have you ever sold anyone a typewriter?'

'Funny you should ask that,' said the witness.

'Why is it funny?'

'Because that's what 'e arst me.'

'Who?'

' 'Im,' and he pointed to Mr Richmond.

'Never mind about him for the moment,' said the judge. 'Have you ever sold anyone a typewriter?'

'Well—I did once't as a matter of fact.'

'How long ago?'

'Dunno.'

'Try and think.'

'Dunno.'

'You must have some idea.'

'Dunno.'

'But you must.'

'If you say so, my Lord.'

'It isn't a question of if I say so or don't say so—you must have some idea when you sold it. Was it last week?'

'Oh, no, before that.'

'Was it ten years ago?'

'Weren't as long ago as all that.'

'Well, then, it was some time between a week and ten years ago?'

'Dunno.'

'But you do know. You've just said so.'

' 'Ave I, my Lord? It's me ignorance I expect.'

'Did you sell it a fortnight ago?'

'Before that.'

'Was it five years ago?'

'Not as long as that.'

'Then it was some time between five years and a fortnight?'

'Dunno.'

'Perhaps you'd continue, Mr Stanmore,' said the judge. 'Whether this witness is as stupid as he tries to make out I don't know, but he's certainly enjoying himself—and if I find out he's trying to be funny he'll be sorry for it. I'm warning you, Mr Brown. Just you answer the questions and don't try to be clever, or you may not go back home tonight.'

'I never wanted to come at all, my Lord, only 'e said 'e'd make me if I didn't.'

'Now, Mr Brown, was it three weeks ago?' continued Stanmore.

'Before that.'

'A year ago?'

'Not so long as that.'

'Then it was between three weeks and twelve months ago?'

'Dunno.' Then—just before Stanmore asked his next question he went on:

'If you really want to know, it was about six months ago.'

'Why didn't you say so before?' asked the judge.

'Wasn't arst if it was six months ago.'

'You were asked when it was, and you could have said six months.'

'I 'ave, my Lord.'

'But not till you'd been asked a large number of unnecessary questions. You could have answered the question long ago.'

' 'Ow long, my Lord—between a week and five years?'

The judge looked severely at the witness.

'I shan't warn you again,' he said.

The witness started to leave the witness box.

'Come back—what are you doing?' asked the judge.

'I thought you said you weren't going to ask me no more questions.'

'I said nothing of the kind. Stay where you are.'

' 'Ow long for, my Lord? I got me barrer outside.'

'Till I tell you to go. Now, you sold a typewriter to someone about six months ago. Is that the typewriter?'

The judge pointed to Richmond's typewriter, which was an exhibit in the case and was on a table in the court.

'Could 'ave been, but I don't know much about such things.'

'Where had you got it from?' asked Stanmore.

'I bought it.'

'From whom?'

'A man.'

'What was his name?'

'Never arst.'

'Where was the man?'

' 'Ow d'you mean, where was 'e? On the pavement, same as me.'

'What pavement—where?'

' 'Ow should I know?'

'You were there.'

' 'Course I was there. He sold it me, didn't 'e?'

'Well, as you were there and as you bought it from him you can say what particular pavement you were standing on when he sold it to you.'

'Well, I can't—see.'

'Why not?'

'Now, look, guv'nor, you ain't never owned a barrer, 'ave yer?'

'Don't ask counsel questions. Just answer his,' said the judge. 'Why can't you say where you bought the typewriter?'

'Well, it's like this 'ere. I goes all round London with me barrer, and I calls on 'ouses to see if they've got anything to sell. And if they 'ave and the price is right, I buys it—and if they 'aven't I don't. And I can no more tell you where I bought anything six months ago than I can tell you where me mother was born and she lived in Putney.'

'But surely it was such an unusual purchase you can remember where you got it?'

'Weren't no more unusual than a lot of other things I've bought. Got a monkey once. And a parrot. In a cage. I've 'ad pictures, and dustbins, and corsets—eiderdowns, tins, saucepans, old iron, lead, flower-pots——'

'Yes, yes,' said the judge, 'but only one typewriter.'

'S'right,' said the witness, 'and I won't buy no more if it's going to cause me all this trouble. Lost arf a day as it is.'

'At any rate,' said Stanmore, 'you can tell us how you came to buy it. Was it offered to you and, if so, by whom? Did you go into the house and see it first, or was it brought to the door? Was it a man or a woman? Who carried it to your barrow? How did you pay for it, and so forth?'

' 'Ow am I supposed to answer all that lot?'

'Well, we'll take them one at a time. Did you call at a house?'

'I might 'ave, or 'e might 'ave come out. I give a shout— see, like this,' and, before he could be stopped, the witness gave a very good example of the rag and bone man's cry.

'Be quiet,' said the judge. 'Don't make that horrible noise here.'

'Sorry, my Lord, thought you'd like to 'ear it.'

'So you don't remember if you rang the bell or knocked on the knocker and asked if they'd anything to sell, or if someone came out and asked you in response to your cry?' asked Stanmore.

'S'right.'

'Do you remember if you went inside a house to look at a typewriter, or if it was brought to you outside?'

'They don't often arst me inside, think I might slip something in me pocket . . . or leave something be'ind.'

'So probably he brought it to the door and said something like "Could you do with this?" or "What'd you give for this?" '

'S'right.'

'And then you said something like—"how much d'you want?" '

'That's right, guv. It wasn't you, I suppose?'

'No, it wasn't me.'

'No offence. I just wondered like, seeing as you seem to know all the answers.'

Stanmore sat down, and Brent got up.

'Do you really remember anything about the transaction?' he asked.

'I just told you.'

'Yes, but do you really remember selling a typewriter to anyone?'

'I wouldn't be 'ere if I didn't, would I?'

'There might be a mistake, mightn't there? This man came up to you and said you'd sold him a typewriter, didn't he?'

'He didn't say nothing at first, 'e just looked at me until I arst 'im if 'is eyes was tired.'

'What did he say then?'

' 'E arst me if I remembered 'im.'

'What did you say?'

'I arst him 'oo 'e was. Can't expect to remember a bloke unless 'e tells you 'oo 'e is, can you?'

'What did he say?'

' 'E turned round and said—"never mind 'oo I am—'ave you ever seen me before?" '

'And what did you say?'

'I turned round and said "wot are yer after?" '

'And what did he say?'

' 'E turned round and said 'e just wanted ter know if I remembered seeing 'im before.'

'Well—what happened after that?'

'I turned round and said I couldn't rightly say.'

'Were both of you turning round all the time?' asked the judge. 'It must have been a pretty odd sight.'

'And what happened then?' went on Brent.

' 'E turned round and arst me if I'd ever sold 'im a typewriter.'

'And after you'd turned round what did you say?'

'I didn't turn round—I was facing 'im all the time like.'

'Very well. What did you say?'

'I turned round and said . . . Oh, I see what you mean, guv —just a manner of speaking as you might say. I told 'im I 'ad sold a typewriter about six months ago. And 'e said, "Well, I bought one six months ago, and I thought you was the man." '

'Yes?'

'Then he arst me if I'd ever sold a typewriter before or since and I turned round . . . I said "No." '

'Then what happened?'

' 'E arst me if I'd come and give evidence like—said 'e was in a jam and nobody believed 'e'd bought a typewriter. So 'ere I am.'

'Did you require a lot of persuading?'

' 'Ow d'you mean?'

'Did he offer you anything for coming?'

'Well, 'e said I wouldn't lose by it. Nothing wrong in that, is there?'

'What did you understand by not losing by it?'

'I thought 'e'd make up what I lost by coming.'

'And has he?'

' 'E gave me a couple of quid, and said 'e'd give me some more when it was over.'

'How much do you expect?'

'I don't expect nothing, guv—but if 'e don't play the game I'll 'ave a thing or two to say.'

'And what will it cost him in your view to play the game?'

'That depends, don't it?'

'On what?'

'Whether 'e goes in the nick. That's why 'e gave me the two pounds, in case I didn't see 'im no more.'

The witness looked towards the dock.

'What are the chances, mate?' he asked cheerfully.

'Behave yourself,' said the judge. 'I've a good mind to fine you for contempt as it is.'

'Don't do that, please, me Lord. It'd be hard on 'im,' and he pointed to the man in the dock.

' 'E'd 'ave to pay it back. Said 'e'd see I didn't lose nothing.'

'And if I sent you to prison?' asked the judge.

'Cost 'im ten quid a week, me Lord.' He thought for a moment and added: ' 'Ow long would it be for, me Lord?'

'Never mind,' said the judge. 'I've had enough of this nonsense. Any more impertinence from you and I'll commit you at once.'

The witness said nothing, but looked up at the ceiling. The judge wondered whether that could be interpreted as impertinence, but decided to give him the benefit of the doubt.

The day ended with the witness still in the box.

'Well,' said Mr Richmond to Stanmore, after he had been released on bail, 'what did you think of him?'

'He's some help, I suppose, but it's another coincidence.'

'It'd be more of a coincidence if it weren't me he'd sold the typewriter to. Just imagine my stopping by chance a man who had sold one typewriter in his life—and not to me. That'd be as incredible as any of the other coincidences.'

'The trouble is,' said Stanmore bluntly, 'that the judge and jury may believe that your Mr Brown is a put up job. I must say,' he added, 'that if it is he did it very well. But there remains the extraordinary series of coincidences, and your Mr Brown can't say where he got the machine from.'

'Then d'you think it would have been better if I hadn't found him?'

'Oh—no, I wouldn't say that,' said Stanmore.

Miss Clinch went to see her elderly mother.

'What's the matter?' said the old lady sharply. 'What can't be cured must be endured.'

'It will not be endured, Mother,' said Miss Clinch. 'Not by me. Not that I think prison will cure either Mr Richmond or his performing witness.'

She told her mother about the day's evidence.

'Well,' said the old lady, 'you mustn't let it upset you. That don't do no good to no one, as your father used to say. And he knew what he was talking about.'

'I'm not a bit upset, mother, but I do hate the thought of the truth not being believed.'

'What is truth?' asked the old lady.

'Something that has no connection with Mr Richmond. I don't blame him for struggling, but he oughtn't to drag other people into it.'

'Be done by as you would,' said the old lady.

'What's that got to do with it?' asked Miss Clinch.

The old lady thought for a moment.

'I don't rightly know,' she said. 'It seemed to come in, but now you mention it I don't know where.'

Mr Tewkesbury spoke to Stanmore before he left.

'I must apologize, sir, for the lack of a proof of Mr Brown's evidence. But, between you and me, sir, it was as well you did not have it. The evidence came out fresher, if I may say so. There's many an honest witness, sir, who looks as though he'd perjure away anyone's life or reputation, just because he's seen a solicitor. Don't think I'm decrying my own profession, sir, but you don't want a proof from an honest witness. Now there are witnesses, sir, from whom a proof is most important, but they're very different from the honest fellow we've just seen. Are those your views, sir, may I ask?'

'I think I may say,' said Stanmore, 'that we have lost nothing by your not being able to take a proof.'

'That's most gratifying, most gratifying. I think that calls for a slight celebration, sir, of which—if you will excuse me—I will now partake.'

And Mr Tewkesbury moved away.

CHAPTER ELEVEN

Out of Order

'THE time is ten minutes past nine,' said the wireless announcer.

'I must be off,' said the judge.

'Will the case end today?' asked Vivienne.

'Oh, good Heavens no. It's good for a day or two more at least.'

'Here is a police announcement,' went on the announcer. 'The series of daring daylight robberies which have recently been committed in as far distant places as Cumberland and Somerset are believed to have been committed by a man who has a very fast car.'

'They think of everything,' murmured Vivienne.

'One of his methods of gaining admission is to pretend that he has come to repair the telephone. The public are accordingly warned to require the production of Post Office authority before they admit anyone purporting to come on such an errand. They are also warned that the man is believed to be dangerous.'

'Well,' said Vivienne, 'how does one require a dangerous man to prove his identity without risking that he'll prove it all too well?'

'What's that?' said the judge.

'Oh—nothing. Just a police message. Good-bye, darling. Don't worry about me any more. I'm going to be a really good, careful judge's wife in the future. You watch me.'

'Don't be frightened. I won't,' he said, and kissed her good-bye. A moment later she heard the car drive away and went to the telephone and had half an hour's conversation with Sally Brent. They discussed their husbands, their clothes, their gardens and some of their friends. On the whole the clothes and gardens came out best. She had not long finished the conversation when there was a ring at the bell. She answered it. A pleasant-looking man of about thirty-five, carrying a black bag, was at the door.

'Good morning,' he said, 'I've come to repair the telephone.'

Vivienne almost fainted at the shock. She had only just used it. This must be the man mentioned by the police. She was terrified, but just managed to summon up enough strength to remain standing. But her head swam for a moment and she couldn't speak. At last she heard herself say:

'But it's not out of order.'

The man remained standing outside the door.

'That's funny,' he said. 'There must be some mistake. Let me look.'

He took out a small note-book from his pocket. Vivienne began to recover. It was just one of those coincidences.

'But this is Snow Cottage, isn't it, madam?' he asked, after looking at his book.

'Yes.'

'Well—that's what I've got here. Are you sure it's all right? These things go wrong all of a sudden sometimes.'

'But I was only just using it a few minutes ago.'

'Were you really, madam? How extraordinary. I suppose it must be a mistake.'

He moved forward slightly and put his foot so that she could not shut the door on him. All her terror returned.

'Hadn't you better go then?' she asked.

'Yes, of course, madam,' he said without moving. 'Pity to keep anyone with a phone out of order waiting. Everyone complains of the phone when they've got it, but they complain all the more when it goes wrong.'

She tried to smile.

'Yes, they do, don't they?' she said, with a nervous laugh.

He looked at his notebook again.

'But here it is, madam. Plain as life. Snow Cottage. Someone's going to get into trouble over this. Hope it won't be me.'

'It's not your fault,' she said ingratiatingly.

'Well—they might say it was. Someone's got to carry the can home. Look, madam, d'you mind if I just come in and have a word with the operator. She may be able to put me right.'

'It's a he, not a she.'

'Oh—is it? I've only just come here.'

'I'd be very glad if you'd go,' said Vivienne, as authoritatively as she could.

'Well, of course I will, madam, but it would be a kindness if you'd just let me have a word with the operator. I should be most grateful. Might save me quite a long journey.'

'Can't I do it for you?' she asked.

'Oh—certainly, madam, if you don't mind. Just say it's the engineer and ask her—I mean him—whose line is out of order. It's very good of you, madam.'

He remained standing by the door but made no attempt to come into the house. Her fears started to disappear. If he were a criminal he'd never let her go to the telephone. She could call for help. She started to walk to the telephone, and as she walked she wondered what to say. If she asked for help it would make her look ridiculous if he were a genuine post office engineer. But if she didn't and he weren't! What was she to do? She ought to have asked for his post office authority, or whatever they carry with them. She couldn't do that now. Anyway, it was no good. If he were genuine he'd produce it and if he weren't he'd knock her on the head or do anything.

'May I come in?' he said.

There were several yards between them now, and she was near the telephone.

'Of course,' she said, but moved more quickly.

He stepped into the room.

'Quite chilly,' he said, and closed the door and stood just inside it. That decided her. Whether I make a fool of myself or not, I'm going to ask for help, she said to herself. He won't dare to do anything when he hears me do that. There must be a police car with wireless somewhere. These things can be done so quickly. But she felt a chill inside when she realized that in fact no one could get to her in time if the man attacked her at once. There was nothing for it. She'd call for help as soon as the operator answered. She reached the telephone and lifted the receiver. The operator normally took a little time to answer. She waited as patiently as she could, but after a few seconds— much less time than she normally waited—she couldn't stand the strain. She moved the lever up and down—first slowly . . . then more quickly. 'Hullo,' she said once or twice. She moved the lever again and still again. The man watched her from the door. Was he smiling faintly? He must have seen her panic. If he smiled did that mean he was genuine and, being an unkind sort of person, thought it rather amusing? Or did it mean he was the wanted man? She started to move the lever more frequently and to say 'hullo' more often. Still the operator did not reply. Eventually she became almost frantic.

'Hullo, hullo, hullo—exchange, exchange, operator—hullo —operator—operator—can't you hear me—hullo, it's urgent— hullo, hullo.'

She worked the lever up and down quite feverishly; she was getting out of control.

'It looks as though I was right, madam,' said the man. 'It shouldn't take all that time.'

'But I've only just been using it,' she said. 'I know it's in order. They take a very long time to answer sometimes.'

'Apparently,' he said. 'Lucky there isn't an emergency. Wouldn't be much use in case of fire—or anything of that sort.'

He still remained quite calmly where he was.

Vivienne continued to speak into the mouthpiece, and move

the lever up and down. She was now becoming almost hysterical.

'If I may say so, madam,' he said, 'you're not giving the operator much of a chance to reply. Don't you think it would be better if you stopped flashing? She can't reply half the time, can she?—sorry, he,' he corrected himself.

Vivienne took his advice and waited for the operator to answer. There was complete silence in the room for about fifteen seconds, though it seemed more like a minute to Vivienne.

'Hullo—hullo,' she said. Still no answer. She started to move the lever again. Still no result. The operator had never taken so long to answer before. Having a cup of tea probably. It was outrageous. She'd speak to her husband about it and he'd do something. Suppose this were a real emergency. These operators! What do they care?

'Operator, operator,' she almost shouted. And then, after she had in fact been trying the telephone for at least five minutes, she realized with terror that it must be out of order.

'Oh—my God!' she said. 'It's quite dead.'

'Dead, is it?' he said. 'How lucky I'm still here. If I hadn't been so pressing I might have gone away. Shall I come and try to see what's wrong?'

He still stood by the door.

She could only say: 'Oh—my God!'

'Don't worry, madam,' he said. 'It's not as bad as all that. May be something quite slight which I can put right in a jiffy.'

'I'll try it again. Perhaps it's the exchange,' she said desperately.

'Of course,' he said. 'I'm not in any particular hurry.'

Again she tried moving the lever and hullo-ing, but all to no purpose.

'Perhaps he's been taken ill all of a sudden,' he suggested. 'If you'd allow me—I could tell if the line is dead.'

'No, thank you,' she said. 'I don't think I want it repaired today.'

'Seems an awful waste—my being here and not at least trying to put it right.'

'Well—I don't want it put right . . . please go—please go away at once.'

'But they'll think I'm out of my senses, madam. Send me to put it right—find it out of order—and leave it without doing a thing. I should certainly get into trouble for that.'

'But I'll tell them it's my fault, and that I didn't want to be disturbed.'

'But supposing something happened to you, madam, you were ill or something, I mean—and you couldn't tell them . . . I might get the sack.'

'I can't help it. Please go. Please go!' she raised her voice as she repeated it.

He scratched his head.

'Well, this really is very odd,' he said. 'The oddest thing I've ever come across. You seemed all upset when you found the phone was out of order, and now you've got me here you don't want me to do anything. It beats me. Are you feeling quite well, madam?'

'No—I'm not. So please go.'

'Shall I ring for a doctor then, madam?' he said. 'Oh—no, of course, I forgot . . .'

He paused for a moment and then went on:

'Ah, I've got it—you're suddenly frightened of being alone in the house with a strange man.'

'Who said I was alone?' she asked.

'Well—after all the fuss you've kicked up, madam, if you'll forgive the expression, I should have thought anyone else would have come along to see what it was all about.'

'What do you want?' she asked, as boldly as she could.

'Want, madam? Just to do my duty and repair the telephone. May I come and inspect the instrument?'

'I can't stop you.'

'What an odd way you talk, madam, if you'll forgive my saying so.'

He started to walk towards the telephone. Suddenly he stopped.

'Oh—good Lord,' he said. 'I've got it. You've been listening to that police broadcast. I heard it in my car—in my van, I mean. Enough to frighten anyone. All alone in a lonely house and the telephone has to go wrong just after a broadcast like that. I expect someone's been trying to get you and failed, and reported your line out of order. These failures are intermittent sometimes, you know. That's why you were able to speak a little while ago and why you can't now. But I'm sorry you've had such a fright.'

Her confidence started to return.

'Then you're not——' She hesitated so long that he asked enquiringly:

'Yes?'

'Then you're not——'

'Not the man they mentioned in the broadcast—you mean, madam?'

'Yes,' she said, 'I *was* frightened—I thought you were.'

He laughed. In relief she laughed too. The laughter became infectious and they both laughed uproariously. Eventually she stopped.

'It *is* a relief,' she said.

'What is, madam?'

'That you're not he.'

'Well, madam,' he said, 'the really amusing thing about it—this'll really make you laugh—the really amusing thing is . . . but let me try the telephone first.'

He went to the receiver and picked it up. After moving the lever several times, he struck the mouthpiece smartly several times.

'Oh—no,' he said, after his swift examination, 'it's plain what's happened here. The line's been cut.'

'But how could that be? I tell you I was speaking a few minutes ago.'

'Well—then it's been cut since then.'

'Extraordinary.'

'Isn't it? But I was telling you—it really is amusing . . . you remember what I was saying a few moments ago?'

'About your not being the man in question?'

'Yes—that was it. Well—the odd thing is that I am, as a matter of fact.'

She said nothing for a moment. Then—'You're joking,' she said.

He laughed.

'Well, which way do you want it, madam? When I say I'm from the telephone service you think I'm a criminal, and when I say I'm a criminal you think I'm from the telephone service. Which way do you want it?'

'I shall report you for this. It's an outrageous way to behave.'

'Well, madam, I agree—it would be if I *were* from the telephone service—but, you see, I'm not.'

She looked at him but could say nothing.

'That explains everything,' he went on, 'doesn't it?'

Everything felt unreal. This couldn't be happening to her. She still clung to the idea that he was merely a buffoon—or, and another thought struck her—a mad telephone engineer. But then the telephone *was* out of order. He must be the wanted man. He interrupted her thoughts.

'Come along now and sit down and have a talk,' he said, sitting down himself on a couch. 'I always prefer a talk with my customers first. It prevents misunderstandings.'

She stood where she was.

'Do come,' he said. 'It's just as safe here as there. After all— I could come and fetch you. Come along, now.'

She made herself move towards him.

'That's better. Come and sit down. Much more comfortable.'

She came and sat next to him.

'Who are you, and what do you want?' she made herself ask.

'That's better. Found your voice. I think you're doing very well on the whole. Some of them faint.'

'I wish I could.'

'Oh—no,' he said. 'Don't do that. That's really dangerous. You see, I never know when a person's going to come out of a faint. It's so embarrassing to be disturbed in the middle of a job. So if you faint I——'

He broke off, and pulled a spanner out of his pocket.

'I make it sort of permanent, see?' he added.

'Of course you don't feel it—which is something. But then even if you're awake you don't feel it for long. There is a point there. If I get you in the right spot you're out first time. But if you put up a show, it stands to reason I may hit the wrong place, and that can be a very messy business. So I always advise customers to co-operate. Now, there's a spot just below the neck where, if you keep still, I can guarantee you a knock-out first time—but only if you keep still, mind you. Hope I'm not boring you.'

'Who are you, and what do you want?' she repeated.

'You have got a one-track mind. Who am I? Well—at the moment I'll call myself Dogsbody . . . an appropriate name, don't you think?—Alfred Dogsbody. Don't ask me why Alfred. What do I want? Well—I'm very catholic in my tastes. I like a lot of things.'

'You can take anything you want.'

He looked at her critically.

'Anything?' he said.

'You know what I mean,' she said.

'Pity,' he said. He looked at her again. 'Yes—great pity. Some old witch must have laid a curse on me when I was small. I'm too much of a gentleman. It's a confounded nuisance. I'm always hoping I'll meet the good fairy who'll release the spell. It's a shame to have the mind of a cad and the body of a gentleman. Don't you agree?'

'If you use that spanner on people I should hardly call it the body of a gentleman.'

She was surprised that she could speak so rationally.

'You have a point there,' he said, 'but there's gentlemen

and gentlemen. Now it's one thing to knock someone on the
head with a spanner—that's what you might call an occu-
pational risk. It has to be done. Got to live, you know. But
there are worse things than using a spanner and, while my
mind is all set on doing them, my confounded body refuses—
like a horse at a jump. My mind's the rider and my body's
the horse. Must have been disqualified long ago for three
refusals. You'll be about the thirty-fourth I should think. Not
all as good-looking as you, though, if I may say so.'

'What are you going to do? Someone may be here any
moment,' she said.

'Oh—who?'

She thought hastily.

'A tradesman, perhaps.'

'He'll go away if you don't answer. Anyone else?'

'I've got a friend coming to see me,' she lied.

'Not bad,' he said, 'but you should have said that first.
Look,' he added, after a pause, 'it'll be much more sensible
to tell me the truth about things. I can usually tell when you're
lying. And if you start playing tricks with me I'm liable to get
awkward. My body responds to that sort of call from my
mind.'

'What do you want me to do,' she asked, after a short pause.

'That's better,' he said. 'Well, first of all, I'd like your keys
and then I'd like you to tell me where everything is. Sometimes I like a conducted tour but on the whole in your case I'd
prefer to go by myself.'

She opened her bag and started to look for her keys.

'Have you a safe?' he asked.

'No.'

'Just as well, I suppose. Your husband would have the keys
and I'd always be wondering what was in it. Much jewellery?'

'A little.'

'Good. In your bedroom?'

'Yes.'

'That's probably all I'll want. That and any spare cash. If

you'll let me have your bag I'll probably be able to sort things out for myself. Thank you.'

She handed over the bag. He got up and started to walk across the room.

'What'll you do while I'm ransacking your bedroom?'

'Stay here.'

'Do you really think I believe that? You'll scuttle out of the front door just as fast as your little feet can carry you, won't you, now?'

'I suppose I would,' she admitted. 'Hadn't you better take me with you?'

'I tell you, I don't want to. Too disturbing. Might take my mind off the job.'

He looked at her for a moment.

'Rather an impasse, isn't it? And another thing that worries me. As soon as I've gone you'll run off to the police and later on, if I'm unlucky, you'll be able to identify me. That's awkward, isn't it?'

She suddenly felt terrified. Previously he had replaced the spanner in his pocket. Now he had brought it out again.

'But I won't—I promise I won't.'

'They all do that,' he said, 'but even if you mean it now— which I doubt—as soon as you've got your husband and the police round you'd break it. I don't altogether blame you. Quite reasonable in the circumstances. But it puts me in an awkward position, don't you see? As a professional man I can't afford to take risks.'

'But if you . . . if you—did anything to me,' she said, 'and you were caught, it would be much worse for you.'

'That's quite true, but who could prove it—except you? With all my escapades up to the moment, I'd get a pretty stiff sentence anyway. With the death penalty pretty well abolished, I couldn't get any more if I disposed of you—and a dangerous possibility of identification would have been avoided.'

'Can't you think of me at all? Can't you think of anyone but yourself?'

'What's the good of having the mind of a cad if I thought of anyone except myself?'

'You don't sound or look the sort of person who'd kill someone in cold blood.'

'Murderers seldom look the part, unless they've got prison clothes on. They make anyone look criminal. If you dressed up all the members of the Athenæum in prison clothes and sent them walking round a prison yard, everyone would say that they were obvious criminals—most of them morons and sub-human. And vice versa. If you put half a dozen regular occupants of Pentonville into judge's robes and put them on the Bench, everyone would say that they looked the part.'

'You don't talk like a man who'd—who'd do the sort of things you're suggesting. I'm sure you aren't.'

'That's where I'm afraid you're wrong. You cling to the hope that I'm not. Very natural. I'd do the same in your position.'

'Please don't . . . please don't. I'll promise anything—and I'll really keep my word. I'm happy. I'm young. I want to live. You can't be so brutal.'

'Personally, I'd be very glad to oblige you. But it can't be done, I'm afraid.'

He came towards her with the spanner.

'Now, remember what I said before. If you make a fight for it, it'll be most unpleasant, and you haven't a chance. If you leave it to me and co-operate, I'll guarantee you an almost painless exit.'

Just as she was trying to make up her mind what to do, they were both interrupted. The front door bell rang. He held up his finger to her, and brought a revolver out of his pocket.

'Let it ring,' he whispered.

After half a minute the bell rang again. Then again, and still again.

'Confound it,' he whispered. 'Now, look . . . you go and answer it and get rid of the man. I'll be watching you from this doorway. No nonsense, or I'll dispose of you both. Don't forget. I'm a professional.'

He moved quietly to the door leading out of the room, and went outside it, leaving it very slightly open. Vivienne went to the front door. There was a man standing there. She did not know him.

'Good morning, madam,' he said. 'I've come to repair the telephone.'

Thank God, she said to herself. Her husband must have tried to ring her and found it out of order and reported it . . . just as the man had said, but it was true this time. But she wasn't out of the wood yet—not by a long way. If she made a false move they might both be shot. But it was a relief to have someone with her. She wasn't alone any longer. But what was she to do? If she dashed out with the telephone man, the man behind the door might shoot. If she brought the telephone man in, they would both be powerless to do anything. Her dilemma was solved for her, however.

'D'you mind if I come in, madam? It's a bit draughty here, and I've had a bit of a cold. Thank you so much.'

He almost pushed his way in and shut the door.

Well, that was that. There was nothing to be done about it. Under her breath she whispered:

'There's a man with a revolver behind the door.'

'I beg your pardon? D'you mind speaking up a little, madam? I'm slightly deaf.'

'Isn't that very awkward in your job?' she said, in her normal voice.

'Not really,' he said. 'As a matter of fact, it doesn't make the slightest difference.'

'How odd,' she said. 'I should have thought that it would have been difficult for you to test lines.'

'I don't test lines, madam.'

'Well—whatever it is you do.'

'Doesn't affect me at all really. What's up with the telephone, anyway?'

'I think the wire's broken or something.'

'How very odd. That really is odd.' He laughed. 'D'you know, madam, I expected you to tell me there was nothing wrong at all.'

'What do you mean? Someone's reported the line out of order—that's what you said, isn't it?'

'Yes—that's what I said, but as a matter of fact it isn't true.'

'What on earth are you playing at then? Why did you come here?'

'I told you I'd come to repair the telephone.'

'I know you did, but if you didn't know it was out of order why did you come—and who sent you?'

'I sent myself as a matter of fact. Anyone else at home, by the way?'

She hesitated.

'No.'

'Good. Then I'll sit down if you don't mind.'

'Aren't you from the Post Office?'

'I'm afraid it's becoming increasingly obvious that I'm not.'

'Then who on earth are you, and what do you want?'

'Did you hear a police message broadcast earlier this morning?'

'Yes—I did, as a matter of fact.'

'Well—that's me, I'm afraid. Awfully sorry, but there it is.'

'But—but . . . that's impossible,' she said.

'Not only not impossible—but a solid fact. Here I am. You can see me. You can touch me. Go on—touch me. I'm real.'

She backed away from him. What *was* all this? There couldn't be two of them. And yet it looked as if there were. And both had to come to her house. Perhaps they'd kill each other. But she might get shot in the process.

'Come on—touch me.'

He took her by the arm and placed her hand on his knee.

'That's me,' he said. 'Feel it? No spooks about me. Solid

flesh. A bit too much of it, perhaps, but there it is. One must eat. Satisfied I'm not a ghost?'

He released her hand.

'What do you want?' she asked.

'Give you three guesses.'

'I'm not much good at guessing.'

'You don't have to be. Your money or your life—or possibly both, that's me. The modern Dick Turpin. But it's more comfortable these days. No perishing rides to York. Go by car if I want to. Fast car I think they said on the wireless. Well, it isn't bad. Get up to ninety on a decent stretch. There aren't enough of them in this country. Give me the German roads. It's worth letting her out on them.'

The thing was so preposterous that Vivienne could have laughed if she had not been so frightened. So there were two of them. That was why there had been incidents such a long way apart. And they both had to come to her. Could she turn it to her advantage? How? What was the first man going to do? If they fought each other might she be able to get away in the middle? Should she tell the second man boldly of the presence of the first? That would be too dangerous. He might shoot them both at once. Should she try to provoke the second man to bring out his revolver, if he had one? She supposed he had. Oh—why wasn't it just a dream? She'd read the papers with interest when Soho gangsters were all the rage. How awful it must be, she had thought, never to know if someone would jump out from an alleyway and slash your face. But they didn't seem to do it to women. Or did they? Soho thugs couldn't conceivably be chivalrous. But these two men didn't seem like what she'd imagined ordinary gangsters were. If she'd met them at a cocktail party they wouldn't have appeared in the least out of place. But this was no cocktail party. Or could she make it one? Could she conceivably make them drunk? Well— there was no harm in trying. Unless she did something she was caught. She couldn't make things worse for herself by trying, if she were careful.

'Would you like a drink?' she said eventually.

'That's very civil of you,' said the second man. 'Where d'you keep them?'

'In that cupboard.'

'O.K. then. Thank you. A straight whisky if you have such a thing would be most acceptable. But don't try and bolt in the process. I played full back at school and I was quite good at a flying tackle.'

She walked slowly and deliberately towards the cupboard. 'Where were you at school?'

'St Giles, as a matter of fact.'

'St Giles?' she repeated, 'I've never heard of it, I'm afraid.'

The internal door opened and the first man stepped in with his revolver ready for action.

'Never heard of it?' he said, with a show of annoyance, 'that's ridiculous. We won the Ashburton Shield one year.'

'Who the hell are you?' said the second man, but he had not had time to bring out any weapon.

'You weren't at Gillies,' said the first man.

'I was.'

'When? In Tupper's time?'

'Yes.'

'Now—don't try anything funny. But I want to know about this. What was the matron's name?'

'Agatha.'

'Aunt Agatha. So you were there. What's your name?'

'Not with ladies present,' said the second man. 'At present it's Smith, but that wouldn't convey much, would it? D'you remember E. O. Smith, by the way—the chap who won the mile when he was fifteen?'

'I'll say I do. I used to pace him.'

'Then you're Makepeace. I thought I saw a likeness to someone, as you came in. Of course you are. Must you keep that thing pointing at me? Point it at her if you must point it somewhere. After all, Gillians don't eat Gillians.'

'God, what a chance,' said the first man. 'We must have a drink on it.'

He put the revolver away.

'Make it two, would you please?' he said to Vivienne. 'If I'm not presuming too much on our short acquaintanceship.'

CHAPTER TWELVE

Still Out of Order

WHILE Vivienne was entertaining her two visitors, the trial of Richmond was proceeding. William Brown was still being cross-examined by Brent.

'Are you really asking the jury to believe that you ever sold anyone a typewriter—the accused or anyone else?'

'I ain't asking nuthink,' replied the witness. 'I didn't never want to come 'ere.'

'Then you admit you didn't sell the accused a typewriter?'

'I don't admit nuthink. Is it fair, my Lord?' and the witness turned towards the judge—'I ain't done nuthink wrong. They shouldn't ask me all these questions. Admit this—admit that—I don't admit nuthink. I don't say nuthink either, that's fair enough.'

'Do you swear you ever sold a typewriter to anyone?'

'There 'e goes again, my Lord. I've 'ad about enough.'

'Just you answer the questions,' said the judge.

'Do you swear you ever sold a typewriter to anyone?' repeated Brent.

'I 'ave.'

'You have what? Sold a typewriter, or sworn you've sold a typewriter?'

'Wot I said. You've got me all confused like. It's all a conflopsion to me.'

'A what?' asked the judge.

'I ain't no scholard.'

'I dare say not. But what was the word you used?'

'When, my Lord?'

'Just now.'

'I used a lot o' words, my Lord. Which one did you mean?'

'Never mind. It's of no importance. It was con . . . con—something.'

'Oh—you mean conflopsion, my Lord. It's the missus' word really, my Lord. I 'ope it's all right to use 'ere.'

'If your wife invented it you can tell her from me that it's a most descriptive word. I'm sorry, Mr Brent, please go on.'

Eventually Brent completed his cross-examination, and the witness left the box after a very short re-examination by Stanmore. The bank manager was then called and Mr Justice Short, unlike Mr Justice Soames, allowed him to give his name and address without interruption. After he had given his evidence, the Court adjourned for the luncheon interval. Mr Justice Short, wanting to speak to Vivienne, tried to telephone her but was told that the line was out of order.

Meanwhile, Vivienne was encouraging the two men to drink. After they had had their third, her spirits began to rise considerably. The men seemed in no hurry and were behaving very differently from the way in which she imagined ordinary housebreakers behaved. These were the amateur cracksmen of the stage. They spent a long time reminiscing over their drinks, and frequently drew Vivienne into the conversation—explaining to her the point of a particular joke and generally treating her as though she were an ordinary hostess who had asked them to drop in for a drink if they happened to be passing. After some time the first man said:

'Well, old boy, I suppose we ought to be going, pleasant as it is here.'

'How about one for the road,' said Vivienne. After the way they'd been talking to her they couldn't surely do anything to her.

'Thanks very much,' said the second man, 'but we must make it snappy. I don't suppose either of us can spare too much time. Which way are you going, by the way?' he asked his colleague.

'Hadn't made up my mind. But we'd better go opposite ways or we might meet again. Toss you for it. Heads I go North, tails you do.'

'O.K.'

They tossed. It was tails.

'Right. North it shall be. We'd better share this one I suppose.'

'Fair enough.'

'What about her?'

The first man hesitated. After a pause he said:

'It seems a shame. Isn't there any other way?'

'How can there be? I agree with you it's a shame. But it's an unfair world, isn't it?' he added to Vivienne.

'Sometimes,' she said.

'I'm afraid this is one of those occasions. I really am awfully sorry. You've treated us awfully well and, if I may say so, you mix a jolly good dry Martini. But business is business. If we let you alone you'll give a perfect description of us to the first policeman.'

'I swear I won't,' said Vivienne, becoming desperate again.

'Even if you mean it now,' said the second man, 'your husband and the police would soon have it out of you. Or p'raps you won't tell them about it?'

'I won't—I promise I won't.'

'Then how will you explain the loss?'

'I can say I went out and found the place broken into—or that I stupidly left the door on the latch . . . or something like that.'

'Are you a good liar, may I ask?'

'Yes—terribly good,' said Vivienne eagerly. 'My husband believes anything I tell him.'

'But he's a judge, isn't he?'

'Yes.'

'Well—that must be because you always tell him the truth.

And after all why shouldn't you? You've never anything to hide. But you wouldn't find he'd believe you if you lied to him. Judges see through people. You can't get away with any old story to them.'

'But you can—really you can,' urged Vivienne. 'And this one's so simple. I can prove it. Look, one of you . . . be my husband, and ask me any questions you like.'

'Well—we must make it a short game—but there's no harm in trying.'

'All right,' said Vivienne. 'How shall we begin?'

'Well, it all depends. Who discovered the loss? You must have, presumably. Then you'd ring the police. They'd get on to your husband. So when he comes home he knows there's been a burglary, or whatever you call it. Right—I'm him. Now tell me—what happened?'

'Well—I just went out for a stroll and to get a few things from the shop, and when I came back I found my jewellery was missing.'

'Lousy, I'm afraid,' said the first man. 'You're obviously too truthful a person, and when it comes to telling a lie you make a hopeless mess of it. "When I came back I found my jewellery missing!" Who on earth would say that—except in a bad play? How did you come to find it missing? Either you'd see traces of someone having entered the house—which made you go and look to see if there was anything missing—or, if there were no traces, you probably wouldn't notice the loss till hours afterwards. Every time you come back from a walk you don't go and have a look to see if your jewellery's all right, do you?'

'Well . . . you tell me what to say.'

'No time, I'm afraid. And even if there were—which there isn't, and even if we trusted you—which we don't, the chances of your being able to get away with it are nil.'

'I promise I won't give you away.'

'Now, look,' said the first man, 'either you're a truthful person or you aren't. If you are, you won't tell lies to your husband just because you've given your word to a couple of crooks. On the other hand, if you're a liar we obviously can't accept your word.'

'A nice piece of logic,' said the second man, 'and unanswerable, I'm afraid.'

'What are you going to do?' asked Vivienne.

Instead of answering, the first man walked across to the drink cupboard and poured out a quarter of a tumbler of gin. He brought it to Vivienne.

'Here, drink this,' he said, 'and you won't notice anything.'

He put the glass in her hands, and she held it fearfully, her hand shaking.

'Come on, drink it up,' said the first man, encouragingly, 'or shall I put a bit of orange in it?'

At that moment the bell rang. The first man ran to the window and peered out cautiously.

'Quick,' he said to the second man. 'Is there a back way?' he asked Vivienne.

'Yes,' she said, 'through there.'

The first man took out a cord and very swiftly tied her hands behind her back. The second man tied her ankles. Then they both rushed out of the room. The bell rang again. Vivienne tried frantically to free herself. They had not made a very good job of it, and it did not take her very long. As soon as she was free she rushed to the door and opened it. A man was there.

'Well, at last, if you'll forgive me saying so, madam,' he said. 'I was just going away. I understand your telephone is out of order.'

CHAPTER THIRTEEN

Mr Tewkesbury at Bay

M R TEWKESBURY, sitting in his office, was gazing contemplatively at an empty whisky bottle, when Miss Winter showed in a Mr Hennings—in the mistaken belief that he was a client.

'How are you, Tewkesbury?' said the caller. 'I'm Hennings. Have you forgotten me?'

'Closer,' said Mr Tewkesbury. 'Can't reach from here.'

Hennings came nearer and took Mr Tewkesbury's hand and shook it.

'We took our finals together, don't you remember?'

Mr Tewkesbury stared at him for a moment.

'That was before you were born,' he said eventually.

'Don't you believe it,' said Hennings. 'We took them together.'

'Well, you wear very well,' said Mr Tewkesbury. 'What d'you take for it? I can't offer you any of my poison. As you can see—it's evaporated.'

'As a matter of fact it was about your—your poison that I've come to see you.'

'I don't mind if I do,' said Mr Tewkesbury.

'Look,' said Hennings, 'The Law Society have asked me to pay you an informal visit. I'm on the Council, you know.'

'Highly honoured,' said Mr Tewkesbury. 'You retiring and they want me instead?'

'Well—no, not exactly.'

'Never mind,' said Mr Tewkesbury. 'I've had worse disappointments in my life. Take things as they come. It's the only way. If one bus won't stop wait for the next. Like that bottle. Wait for the next. Empty things are horrible, whether they're heads or whether they're bottles.'

'Now, look,' said Hennings, 'I've come round to see if I can be of any use.'

'Well,' said Mr Tewkesbury, 'thirty-six shillings at the present moment would be of the most considerable use.'

'The Council are very worried about you.'

'Very civil of them,' said Mr Tewkesbury. 'I can't say that I'm worried about them, but, if I were, thirty-six shillings would put it right.'

'You simply can't go on as you are.'

'How right you are,' said Mr Tewkesbury. 'That must be remedied immediately.'

He rang the bell sharply.

'Miss Tompkins,' he said, when it was answered, 'kindly go round to Roebucks and bring our guest a bottle of the best.'

'Very good, sir——' the girl hesitated. 'Could I have the——'

'Don't be bashful, girl,' said Mr Tewkesbury. 'You want the necessary, the wherewithal, the that-without-which-not—in other words, the cash.'

'Yes, sir.'

'Is the petty cash so petty that you can't find it there?'

'There's only seventeen and fourpence, after I've took my wages.'

'Then the solution is simplicity itself. Don't take your wages. Go home, your chest swelling with pride, and tell your adoring parents that you're not like other girls who take all they can get—that you're a horse of a very different colour, a girl in a thousand, generous, kind, bountiful—in other words that you've not took your wages.'

'But there's the rent, Mr Tewkesbury.'

'Rapacious landlords! Let them wait.'

'And food, Mr Tewkesbury.'

'You eat too much.'

'Oh—no, sir.'

'We'll submit the matter to arbitration. You can rely on Mr Hepplewhite giving a fair decision. Now, sir, would you not say that the young lady ate too much?'

'I would not,' said Hennings, 'and my name is not Hepplewhite.'

'Set aside the award,' said Mr Tewkesbury, 'on the ground of the irrelevance of the last sentence. Technical misconduct. Fresh arbitration before a fresh arbitrator. Ask Mr Roebuck if he'd oblige, and don't be too long. Mr Hepplewhite is not thirsty, but Mr Hennings and I are.'

'Not for me, thank you,' said Hennings.

'Don't bother about that second glass,' said Mr Tewkesbury.

'D'you think I could have a word with you in private?' said Hennings.

'My dear sir, of course. On the production of thirty-six shillings the lady will vanish.'

Hennings reluctantly took out his pocket-book and gave the girl one pound. He did not see why the seventeen and fourpence left in the petty cash should not supply the balance.

'Don't forget to enter it in the book,' said Mr Tewkesbury. 'Open a loan account for Mr Hennings. Will a quarter per cent above bank rate suit you, sir?'

Mr Hennings said nothing until the girl had gone.

'Now, look here, Tewkesbury,' he said. 'The Council will have to take action against you if you don't behave yourself. You're bringing the profession into disrepute.'

'The charge, may I ask?'

'You know perfectly well. Drunkenness.'

'But not in charge of a case, sir, not in charge of a case. I'm bound to admit, sir, between these eight walls, that I have an addiction to the bottle. I like the stuff, sir. I think I may fairly say that I thrive on it. But in charge of a case, never, sir.

Against my principles. The client comes first, sir, the bottle second. A good second, if you like sir, a game second you might say, but second—definitely second, half a length, shall we say, or three-quarters, no need for the camera anyway, the judge can see for himself.'

'He has seen for himself, I'm afraid,' said Hennings. 'You've at least three convictions for being found drunk and incapable.'

'Oh,' said Mr Tewkesbury, 'magistrates aren't what they were, sir. You'd be the first to agree with me about that, sir.'

'I don't agree at all and, even if I did, you're not saying you weren't guilty on each occasion, are you?'

'Ah—sir, you've a good point there. I've been convicted, sir, and it would be idle for me to say I was not guilty if I've been convicted. As you would be the first to agree sir, I feel sure—I was innocent on each occasion, but I was convicted, sir, there's no doubt about it, I was convicted. And, unless Her Gracious Majesty should be pleased to grant me a free pardon —and between you and me, sir, I doubt whether she'll have time to get round to it, sir, until then I must accept the verdict and take my medicine. Which reminds me, sir, she's a long time getting it. Not the Queen, sir, my secretary—my amanuensis, my rod, my staff, my invaluable Miss . . . Miss . . . now what would you say her name was, sir?'

'You called her Miss Tompkins.'

'That doesn't signify, sir. I use the first name that comes into my head. It saves taxing the memory unnecessarily. I take the view, sir, and I've no doubt you'd be the first to agree with me, sir, that there is a limit to the storage capacity of the upper cylinder.'

He tapped his head.

'It stands to reason, sir, it can't hold everything. When it's full and you add something to it, something must go. That's nature's way, sir. Now, sir, I have many serious matters to remember, matters of the greatest possible importance to my clients. But how can I remember them all, sir, if petty, unworthy matters are always intruding? The answer is, sir, that I cannot. And so, sir, I make a point of not remembering anything which is not of the greatest importance. Now my name, sir, is important; I remember that. But your name, sir, if you will forgive me, is of no importance. Whether you are Hennings, or Hepplewhite, or Hollingborne or Hunstanton, you'll know I'm talking to you if there's no one else in the room. And as for the girl's name, there's no one else in the office, so she answers to anything I call her. Her name is Winter, sir. Dear, dear—this is most upsetting . . . I've remembered it. That means I must have forgotten something else. This is most disturbing. You follow what I mean, sir, I hope? It's true that I only remembered her name was Winter because it's one of the Seasons and I first employed her in April, sir. Now, April is not in the winter, sir, and I remember that—as is my wont when employing new staff, I like to start with an air of good humour, of jocularity—I remember saying to her— "Now is the autumn of our discontent made glorious summer by this winter in spring!" I think that rather good, sir. Even the bard himself could only bring in the two seasons. I brought in the four. I hesitated between spring of winter, or winter in spring. But she's a heavy girl, so I chose the latter. She's certainly a slow girl, don't you think, sir. Roebuck's is only two minutes walk. That's how I came to choose this office.'

'I wish you would be serious for a moment, Tewkesbury,' said Hennings. 'It's perfectly true that no client of yours has made a complaint to the Law Society.'

'And if they had, sir, if they had? One can't win every case, sir. Even the best men of our day don't win all their cases. Indeed, sometimes my clients have been most warm in their thanks when I've lost a case for them.'

'I'm not referring to winning or losing cases,' said Hennings. 'I'm referring to your being drunk. And though your clients haven't complained there have been complaints from judges and masters.'

'Not sitting in Court, sir—never in Court.'

'That may be true,' said Hennings.

'Then you're no doubt referring to judges and masters sitting in chambers. Well, sir, it's perfectly true that I have seen a judge or master or two wince a bit when I came near them. And it shows you how sober I was, sir, that I noticed it. I'll be perfectly frank with you, sir—there are no ladies present, I think . . .'

Mr Tewkesbury looked round the room to satisfy himself on the subject. Then he rose and opened a cupboard.

'Good,' he said, on returning, 'they've taken her away. Well, as I was saying, sir, I won't beat about the bush. It's my breath, sir, they don't like it. I once heard a whispered remark, sir—"It's like a public saloon," I heard the judge say to his clerk. I stepped back a pace on that, sir. Didn't want to prejudice my client's case. But may I point out to you, sir, that mine is only one type of breath? Bad teeth, bad digestion can be as noxious as alcohol, sir, and a good deal worse, sir. After all, my breath has pleasant associations, very pleasant indeed.'

'But it can't go on, Tewkesbury, really it can't. You're notorious. The Council will simply have to do something. The convictions alone are a disgrace.'

'There I agree with you, sir. Injustice is always a disgrace.'

'You were convicted, and that's an end of it.'

'That's what I say, sir. I've paid the penalty and that's an end of it. So long as I conduct my practice with my normal propriety, my private affairs are no concern of the Council. If I have the misfortune from time to time to bang my head on the pavement I don't expect a letter of sympathy from the Council—that's not their function—though on the third occasion it might not have been altogether out of place. But as for censure, sir, or threats, I'm amazed, sir. My private life is my own, sir.'

At this point Mr Tewkesbury thumped the desk with his fist.

'You don't dispute that do you, sir?'

'Provided you don't bring the profession into disrepute.'

'What's that you say, sir? Suppose I were involved in a divorce case—suppose I had a wife and she charged me with cruelty—nothing to do with my profession—just knocking her about . . . you know, a woman, a dog and a walnut tree—would the Council have to intervene then, sir? If they did I might have something to say, sir, I might have a great deal to say, sir.'

'Well, as a matter of fact, apart from your drunkenness, you have the reputation of having a very unsavoury lot of clients, and of being prepared to do anything for them—legal or not.'

'Will you repeat that, sir, in the presence of Miss Winter, sir? Confound you, sir, you've made me remember the name again. It's too bad, sir. I wonder what I've forgotten now. Will you repeat it in her presence?'

'Of course I won't. We can't prove anything against you. I'm just giving you a friendly warning.'

'A friendly warning, is it, sir? Insult me to my face and call it a friendly warning. Have you ever heard of insulting words and behaviour, sir? Which would you say are worse, sir, drunk and incapable or insulting words and behaviour?'

Hennings got up.

'I'm sorry,' he said, 'I didn't mean to annoy you. But I'd hoped that if you knew you were skating on very thin ice you might be a bit more careful.'

'I'm past the age of skating, sir, and my only connection with ice is when it's surrounded by whisky. On the rocks, they call it. In that sense I'm often on them and a very pleasant place to be. Indeed if we had a refrigerator here, instead of a safe, I might have offered you one as soon as Miss . . . Miss Tompkins comes back. Good, sir, I've managed to forget her name. Now there'll be room for the confidences of my next client. And there will be room for him in that chair, sir, when you've gone.'

'I'm sorry,' said Hennings, as he ended the interview, 'I've done my best.'

'And what more can one do?' said Mr Tewkesbury. 'My principles exactly. If only they were Miss Tompkins' as well, I should have been more in a mood to meet my next client. It mellows, my dear sir, it mellows. If I have been at all unfriendly, sir, put it down to the slothful Winter—confound it, sir, I've remembered her name again.'

CHAPTER FOURTEEN

Sorry You've Been Troubled

IT was while Mr Tewkesbury was being interviewed by his old acquaintance that Vivienne was talking to the third telephone man. But this time he really was from the Post Office. The judge, on being unable to get through, had asked the engineers to find out what was wrong and put it right. They had not wasted any time in doing so. A judge's telephone may be of considerable importance. At any hour of the day or night a judge can be approached for an urgent order which, if given later, may be given too late. The telephone is a useful link for this purpose.

The line was quickly mended, and the police sent for. Vivienne told them everything as fully as she could. After they'd left she telephoned Sally Brent to describe her dreadful experiences. Sally was most sympathetic.

'It must have been awful,' she said. 'I think you were quite wonderful. Would you like me to come over? I can easily . . . I —hullo, hullo—are you there, Vivienne—hullo, hullo—how extraordinary—hullo—hullo—operator . . . oh, well.'

Sally replaced the receiver, turned on the wireless faintly and sat down near to the telephone. A moment or two later the front door bell rang. She went to the door and opened it. A man was standing there.

'I believe your telephone's out of order,' he said.

'Yes, it is,' she answered. 'But how did you know?'

He pushed his way into the house and shut the door.

'I cut the wire,' he said.

He spoke with a moderately cultured voice, but he was not either of the men who had called on Vivienne.

Sally's reaction was anger rather than fright.

'How dare you!' she said. 'Get out at once.'

'You can see I'm not going to, so why get cross about it?'

'Of all the bloody impudence,' said Sally angrily, and she went up to him and slapped his face hard.

'Now get out,' she said.

The man seemed dazed at first, but he soon recovered. He said nothing, but held both Sally's arms behind her back and slapped her face smartly on both sides several times. Then he let her go.

'If that hasn't calmed you down, I can do it a lot harder. Tantrums won't do any good, and they may do a lot of harm.'

Sally's anger had disappeared. She burst into tears and threw herself helplessly on a sofa.

'That's better,' he said. 'But that won't do any good either. You and I have got some business to do, so pull yourself together and sit up and listen. Come on now, or I'll have to make you.'

Sally did as she was told.

'What do you want?' she asked tearfully.

'First of all—there's no one else in the house, is there?'

'No.'

'Are you expecting anyone?'

'Not for some time.'

'Good. Now look, you're coming round with me while I ransack the house, and I warn you—if there's the slightest bit of nonsense I'll hurt you. Is that plain?'

'Only too plain,' said Sally.

'Right. Now, we'll start in your bedroom.'

She started to lead him to the bedroom when he stopped.

'Look,' he said, 'just in case any one does call, I'm a house agent looking over the place. You've a vague idea of selling it. If you try to give the alarm I'll kill you both. D'you quite understand?'

Sally nodded. As they started to leave the room the front door bell rang.

'Confound it,' said the man. 'Have you been lying to me?'

'I haven't—really I haven't.'

'Well, go to the door and get rid of him. Don't forget I'm covering you both from behind this curtain.'

He stepped behind the curtain, and Sally went to the door. She opened it wide and a man stepped straight in.

'There's a fault on your line. I've come to put it right,' he said.

'What did you say?' she asked incredulously.

'A fault's been reported on your line, and I've come to see to it.'

Before Sally had made up her mind what to do, the man behind the curtain stepped out, holding a revolver.

'Shut the door,' he said, 'and no tricks. This works.'

Sally shut the door.

As she did so she heard the first man laugh.

'Good God,' he said, 'it's the Bosun himself. Where did you spring from?'

Sally turned round and saw that the first man had put away his revolver.

'We're buddies,' he explained to her.

She tried to think that it was a nightmare. Surely she must be imagining it. This was exactly what Vivienne had said had happened to her. They must be the same men, she thought. But she was wrong. They were not. Her first man had gingery hair and her second was going slightly grey. Vivienne's, on the other hand, both had black hair. And it was all their own.

'How did you get into this racket?' asked the second arrival.

'Same as you, I expect. Imitation the sincerest form of flattery. Scotland Yard still thinks there's only one of us. More power to their elbow.'

Sally made a swift decision and rushed for the door. But she was too late. They brought her back and slowly and methodically proceeded to tie her up and gag her.

'I like that tune,' said the ginger-headed man, referring to the wireless. 'What is it?'

'No idea,' said the other. 'D'you know?' he asked Sally.

Sally shook her head.

'I'm sorry about this,' said the second man, 'but there's no alternative.'

At that moment the bell rang. He ran to the window and looked out cautiously. Then he came back and both men ran out of the room. After a moment or two the bell rang again. Sally struggled hard to free herself, but without success. The dance music continued, and again the bell rang. Suddenly the dance music stopped.

'We interrupt the dance music,' said the B.B.C. announcer, 'with a statement from Scotland Yard. Earlier today we broadcast a warning about a man who is gaining admission to houses all over the country by pretending that he has come to repair the telephone. Unfortunately we omitted to add that on no account should this man be admitted into the house without first making sure of his *bona fides*. That is the end of the announcement.'

The dance music was resumed and Sally continued her struggles to get free.

CHAPTER FIFTEEN

Speech for the Defence

MEANWHILE Richmond's trial was drawing to its close and Stanmore was making his final speech to the jury. The proceedings had been interrupted earlier by a police message to the judge. He was told that two men had tried to burgle his house but that his wife was quite all right. He spoke to her on the telephone, but, as there was nothing he could do to help the police and as Vivienne seemed quite well, he decided not to adjourn the case but to go on till the normal hour. Accordingly Brent sat back to listen to Stanmore, while Sally continued her struggles at home.

'Members of the jury,' said Stanmore, 'I am loath to detain you longer than is necessary, but I am sure that you realize how important this case is to my client. Now, what does the case for the prosecution come to? Stripped of sneers at coincidences, I suggest that it comes to very little indeed. First and foremost I remind you that no one has been able—I won't say to prove—but even to suggest by the slightest evidence that two men did not burgle my client's house, knock him on the head and steal a hundred thousand pounds. There is no doubt he had a hundred thousand pounds, there is no doubt that it was the bank manager who persuaded him to insure it; there is no doubt he no longer has the hundred thousand pounds. What is my client's crime then? Buying a typewriter from a barrow boy. That's his crime, members of the jury, but the prosecution call it obtaining or attempting to obtain money by false pretences. A trifle of an exaggeration don't you think,

members of the jury? Do you remember the scorn my learned
friend poured upon this *story* of the barrow boy, as he called it;
how he laughed and invited you to laugh at my client's baldness and lameness, how he sneered at the possibility that the
barrow boy existed in real life? And then we called the man
himself—the man who was supposed only to exist in my client's
imagination. And what does my learned friend do when he's
recovered from the shock? He sneers at the coincidence of my
client finding the witness. Don't you think that's a bit hard,
members of the jury? First they say the witness doesn't exist
and then, when he's produced, they say we oughtn't to have
produced him. Which way do they want it? Of course it was a
coincidence, members of the jury, that my client should happen
to buy this particular typewriter. Of course it was a coincidence
that he should happen to meet the barrow boy during his trial,
but are such coincidences stranger than many of those which
have happened to you? That is, of course, if you believe the
barrow boy is telling the truth. Well, what did you think of
him, members of the jury? He wasn't exactly a helpful witness
from my point of view, was he? I found it difficult enough
to get anything out of him at all. It didn't look, did it, as
though he were trying to help my client? That he was trying
to show off is quite another matter. But either he sold a typewriter to my client or he and my client have entered into a
wicked conspiracy to deceive you. Whatever you may have
thought of Mr Brown, did you think he was that type of man?
Did it seem to you that he was putting on an act? If so, you
may think he had mistaken his vocation. He should be on the
stage. Don't you think that if he and my client had put their
heads together to tell a cock and bull story about this typewriter he'd have given his evidence very differently? Don't you
think he'd have said definitely when and where he sold the
typewriter to my client? Don't you think he'd have been able
to give you perfect reasons for remembering the transaction
and its precise date and place? Isn't that the way alibis are
arranged, members of the jury? I remember hearing the clock

strike because I'd just seen four robins in the garden and then
it struck four. Isn't that the sort of thing on which false alibis
and false stories are based? I don't put forward Mr Brown as a
particularly clever man, nor even as a particularly reliable
man, but was he honest, members of the jury? That's the
question. Was he repeating a piece he'd been told—or paid
by my client to learn, or was he doing his best to remember a
transaction which he'd very nearly forgotten all about? There
it is, members of the jury, it is for you to judge.'

At that stage the judge intervened.

'Mr Stanmore,' he said, 'I suppose you'll be a little time
more?'

'Yes, my Lord.'

'Then I think this will be a convenient moment to adjourn.'

And just about that time Sally was set free. The man who
had come to the door had noticed the cut wire. Having rung
several times, and thinking there might be something wrong,
he had broken into the house. As Brent was on his way home
the police were taking a statement from her.

CHAPTER SIXTEEN

Reflections of Counsel

BRENT felt very cheerful on the way home. He always enjoyed making the final speech. He liked the feeling that no surprises could be sprung on him. At any time during a case, until the evidence is closed, something unexpected may turn up, something which, if it does not completely destroy your own case, may cause you to take drastic steps to repair the damage it does. Even when the evidence is closed, if your opponent has the last word you have to sit and listen to him making points which, if you're lucky and able, you should have answered in advance. But will the jury remember your answers? Your opponent strains every nerve to make the most of his points. It is true you have said: 'My learned friend will shortly say to you that etc., etc. When he does so, however, members of the jury, you will remember etc., etc.' But will the jury remember? Then again you have to think of every conceivable point your opponent may make, good, bad or indifferent. Some points may seem so bad to you that you don't even bother to answer them. But suppose they fool the jury and suppose the judge doesn't notice them? Even if you're very able and very lucky, your opponent may still be able to land some damaging blows to your case and you have to sit and listen with no chance of reply or interruption, unless he mis-states the facts, or says something so unfair that intervention is justified. No, Brent hated listening when his opponent had the final speech, but he had to, just in case he was compelled to interrupt. But when his was the last word it was quite a different matter. Then he was dealing with known quantities. The jury had heard all the evidence and everything that the other side's counsel wanted to say. He could deal with each point at his leisure. It was no question of guesswork. Bit by bit he could destroy the structure which his opponent had built up. It was a satisfying exercise. It was his opponent who then had to grin and bear it, wishing that he had been more prescient and dealt with some point that was going to be made. It was his opponent who would then have to writhe against him while he carried the jury along with him triumphantly. Only the judge stood between him and the jury. It would indeed be nicer to be able to make a speech after the judge's summing up, but that was asking for too much. On the whole judges could be trusted to sort out the sheep-points from the goat-points. That indeed was why he minded far less when his opponent had the last speech if the case were being tried by a judge alone. That was a very different matter. In those cases you could often, if not always, tell which way the judge's mind was working—you could tell the points which weighed with him in your favour and those which weighed with him against you. And indeed it was much easier to interrupt in the middle of your opponent's speech if there were no jury. But you could never tell what a jury was thinking. Indeed, as often as not maybe, they weren't thinking as a jury at all—until they had to consider their verdict. They were all individuals. That short fat man at the back, who seemed profoundly bored, was he taking anything in? The woman who nodded slightly when you made a point and looked at her; did she really know what the point was and, if she did, would the rest of the jury listen to her in the jury room? Appearances are sometimes very deceptive. Is the intellectual-looking man, who seems to follow the proceedings carefully and with perfect understanding, really a bookmaker's clerk working out the odds for some race? Did the man with the Old Reptilian tie notice that one of your witnesses was wearing the same tie and was obviously not entitled to it? Dealing with a jury, Brent always thought, was

most unsatisfactory—unless you had the last word to them.
And on this occasion he had. And it was important that he
should have it too. Stanmore was making a dangerously able
speech, and it needed blowing sky high, as blow it he would.
He made a note of all the points he had made so far. It was a
pity that Stanmore hadn't finished his speech. But he was too
old a hand for that. If the judge had not suggested an adjournment at the time he did, Stanmore would have made sure that
he still had something left to start the next day with. Well, he
could guess pretty well what it would be, and, if there were
something he hadn't thought of, well, he'd be able to deal with
that too. He wasn't in the least vindictive. He did not personally care what happened to Richmond. A case was a case,
and he had to do his best in it. He was an admirable prosecutor,
because his best did not mean that he used every means to
secure a conviction. Not at all. If he had thought his case was
a weak one he would say so. He had even been known almost
to invite a jury to acquit. In the present case, if there were any
reasonable chance that coincidences like those relied on by
the defence could have happened, he would frankly have
admitted it. But they weren't. The case was dead as a door
nail. He mustn't bore the jury, but it was surely time some
reference was made to the lame and bald gentlemen selling
their one and only typewriter to another lame and bald gentleman through the agency of a barrow boy conveniently found
by the lame and bald gentleman on his way to Court. Brent
did not normally make jokes at the expense of people who were
being tried for serious crime. But if ever there were a case
where he was justified in laughing the defence out of Court
this was it. And if he cracked a joke in the process it was fair
enough. The defendant had brought it on himself. An able
man, though, he thought, and quite imperturbable in the
witness box—and with a strong air of sincerity. It was fortunate for the prosecution that he had to appear sincere about
matters which were beyond belief. It was obvious that the
judge thought so too. It was all over bar the shouting. But he

was paid to shout on behalf of the prosecution, and shout he would—though in the quiet, confident tones of a prosecutor who, by his very restraint, would show the inexorable strength of his case. Indeed, his first few words would be uttered in a softness of voice to contrast with the closing violence of Stanmore's oratory. Indeed, if he could pick up something out of Stanmore's last sentence or two and repeat it without the overtones, it would probably be effective. But those are matters for the last moment. Most opponents, however able, usually presented something to you on a plate. He remembered one such occasion, when his opponent had said: 'My learned friend Mr Brent is no doubt going to have a fine old time with the evidence of Mr So-and-So.' To which he said, early in his speech: 'My learned friend has said that I'm going to have a fine old time with the evidence of Mr So-and-So. He's quite right. I am.' Even the judge, who did not particularly like him, had grinned broadly at that sally. Sally—how odd. He'd been thinking of her a good deal lately. Perhaps he hadn't been entirely fair to her. They must have a holiday at the end of this term. A special holiday. To make up.

CHAPTER SEVENTEEN

A Change of Front

H E was horrified when he arrived home. Police cars, ambulance, doctor. Almost as though there had been an air raid. But he was soon relieved from his first panic. Sally's nerves were very resilient and though the doctor was useful—as they often are—the ambulance was unnecessary. He was astounded at the number of police. Even the Chief Constable was there. He knew him slightly.

'Very lucky escape they both had,' he told Brent.

'Both? Who was with her?'

'Of course, you don't know.'

The Chief Constable then explained to Brent that Sally's experiences had been matched by Vivienne's—though Sally's temper had cost her rather more.

'How extraordinary,' said Brent. 'I must get the judge on the telephone—that's if the line's been repaired.'

It had been, and he was soon speaking to Mr Justice Short. First they enquired after each other's wives, and then talked about the astonishing series of events. They satisfied themselves that all four men were different.

'What's so extraordinary,' said the judge, 'is that there were four of these chaps and the police thought there was only one.'

'You've more confidence in the police than I have,' said Brent. 'As a matter of fact it was the obvious solution. Turning up in different parts of the country. He has a fast car, indeed! They might have thought that there might be more than one.

153

Not that that would have helped us. But what's so extra-ordinary is that two of them should choose your house and two mine. Talk of coincidences.'

'I don't think,' said the judge, 'that at the moment we ought to talk about coincidences.'

They finished their conversation and went back to their wives. There's nothing like a good accident to bring people together. A good war makes people realize how fond they are of each other. You don't realize how much you like bread and butter until you can't get it.

The next day Brent realized that it was useless to try to read the paper in the train. Indeed, he did not particularly want to. He was quite prepared to talk about Sally's and Vivienne's adventures. The case of Mr Richmond and his £100,000 took very much a back seat.

'What would you have done if it had been you and not your wife?' he was asked.

'Nothing, I suppose. I certainly wouldn't have had the guts to lash out. What can you do? If a chap's armed you've got to do what he says. It's only on the films that he obliges by putting his weapon down or falling for some kind of childish trick. They have to there, or there wouldn't be a happy ending.'

'Well, I'm glad you've had a happy ending, anyway.'

'Yes—it was a near thing.'

'Think there's any chance of getting the chaps?'

'Your guess is as good as mine. My wife's looked at hundreds of photographs, but none of them seems to fill the bill.'

'What a million to one chance they should follow on each other like that.'

'They say,' said the man next to Brent, 'that if a million monkeys who could type started——'

'Yes, yes, I know,' interrupted Brent, who was uncomfortably reminded of what he'd said to the jury in Richmond's case, 'it's a very extraordinary series of coincidences.'

By the time he had reached the Old Bailey, Brent had resumed thinking about his final speech, but, when he came to deliver it, it was somewhat different from the speech he would have made the preceding day.

'Members of the jury,' he said, 'when I opened this case to you some days ago I said that, if the prisoner were innocent, you were going to hear the most astonishing series of coincidences you had ever heard. Well, now you have heard them, and it is entirely for you to say what you think about them. But as counsel for the prosecution—whose duty it is not to secure a conviction at all costs but to put the arguments for the Crown fairly before you—as counsel for the prosecution I feel bound to say that it is possible that I put the case against the prisoner too high in the first instance. Undoubtedly the coincidences relied upon by the prisoner are strange, but perhaps I underestimated the astonishing coincidences which can and do happen in real life. Perhaps even stranger things do occur than must have occurred in this case if the accused is innocent. I certainly invite you to consider the evidence most carefully and to decide whether you can accept the explanation given to you by the accused for his possession of the incriminating typewriter; but it is, of course, for the Crown to prove its case against the accused, not for him to disprove it. I have, indeed, during this case invited you expressly or by implication to laugh the defence out of Court. I have suggested that in real life—and it is with real life that you are dealing—that in real life such coincidences do not happen, and you may remember that I talked to you about the million monkeys with their million typewriters producing the works of Shakespeare. Well, members of the jury, for reasons which are no concern of yours, I think it is right that I should now put the case differently to you. I suggest that you should consider whether the Crown has satisfied you that the defendant is lying when he says he bought the typewriter from the barrow boy, and that the barrow boy was lying too. If you are satisfied as to these matters, then I invite you on behalf of the prosecution

to find the accused guilty. But if you are not so satisfied your
duty is to return a verdict of not guilty.'

Brent sat down. Stanmore whispered to him:

'Thanks very much. Let's hope the judge follows your lead.'

At that moment the associate spoke to the judge.

'I shall have to rise for a few minutes,' the judge said, after
a short conversation.

Brent and Stanmore went to the robing-room for a cigarette,
while the judge went to see a police inspector in his room.

'I'm sorry to trouble you, my Lord,' said the inspector, 'but
do you think we're justified in holding this man?'

He showed the judge a photograph.

'Lady Short says it's not unlike him, but she can't positively
identify him.'

'What about Mrs Brent?'

'Definitely not, my Lord. She says it's nothing like either of
the men she saw.'

'What is the man you've got. And how did you get hold
of him?'

'Only from the records, my Lord. He's got a very long
record and when we showed his photograph to Lady Short she
felt it might be him. So we had an identification parade. She
just picked him out. But, of course, she only did so because of
the photograph. She says she can't say he *is* the man, but there
is quite a likeness.'

'Did you get him to speak?'

'How d'you mean, my Lord?'

'Did you get him to talk in front of my wife—to see if she
could recognize the voice?'

'No, my Lord, I'm afraid we didn't.'

'Well, I should do so if I were you. You say you're what you
call holding him. Well, you can't do that, you know. Either
you can arrest him or you must let him go. But you ought to
be able to arrange a short conversation, which my wife can
hear, before he actually disappears.'

'Thank you very much, my Lord. We'll do so at once.'

The inspector left and Brent and Stanmore were summoned from the robing-room. Brent put out his cigarette.

'He might have given us time to finish one,' he said. 'That's the trouble with these non-smokers.'

They went back to Court and the judge began his summing up. First of all he explained the nature of the charges against the prisoner, then he reviewed the evidence, after which he dealt with the question of proof.

'Members of the jury,' he said, 'as counsel for the prosecution has told you, it is not for the accused to prove his innocence but for the prosecution to prove his guilt. Now, how must that guilt be proved? It cannot be proved with complete certainty— because you can only be completely certain of something you have plainly seen for yourselves. Each of you knows for certain that you are sitting on this jury. You do not have to be as sure of the prisoner's guilt as that. You can see the reason for that if you think about the matter. If you had to be as certain as that, you would have had to have witnessed the crime, and then you would be a witness and could not be a juryman. It may be that the original juryman in this country was a witness, but we are long past that stage. To be a judge or a juryman sitting on a case one must have no connection with it whatso-ever. Complete impartiality is the modern requirement and has been for many, many years. Well, then, if you cannot have complete certainty what measure of certainty is required? Although different judges may put the matter in different ways, I tell you that the measure of certainty required is that you should be satisfied beyond all reasonable doubt. You must be able to say to yourselves—"I have no doubt but that he is guilty. I am as sure of his guilt as I can be sure of anything which I have not plainly seen for myself." Some people some-times ask: "What is reasonable doubt?" It means what it says, members of the jury; a reasonable doubt is a doubt which is not fanciful, is a doubt which is not based simply on the catch-phrase "Anything may happen"—in other words, it is a doubt which is reasonable. If, for example, the only reason you were doubtful of a prisoner's guilt was because you had not personally seen him commit the crime, that would be a fanciful doubt, an unreasonable one. On the other hand, if you were not sure whether the chief witness for the prosecution, upon whose word the prisoner's guilt mainly depended, was telling the truth—then you would have a reasonable doubt about his guilt and your verdict would be Not Guilty. Use your common sense, members of the jury. Say to yourselves—we cannot have complete certainty in these matters, for the reasons which the judge has mentioned; have we the next best thing to it—are we as sure of the accused's guilt as you can be sure of anyone else's affairs which you have not plainly seen for yourselves? And don't forget, members of the jury, it is for the Crown to prove the prisoner's guilt and, if you have any real doubt about that guilt, he is entitled to be acquitted. So much for the measure of proof. The final question you have to ask yourselves is whether the evidence justifies you in finding that the case has been proved. Now, although this trial has necessarily occupied a good deal of your time, there is really only one question of fact upon which the guilt or innocence of the prisoner depends. If he bought the typewriter as he said he did, he is plainly innocent and is the victim of coincidences— victim in the sense that he has been suspected of and charged with crime in consequence of coincidence. Conversely, if you are satisfied that he did not buy the typewriter from the barrow boy, then I would say—although it is a matter for you to decide, for the facts are for you—that you would be irresistibly led to the conclusion that he was guilty. So far, so good. Satisfied he bought the typewriter from the barrow boy— plainly Not Guilty. Satisfied he has had the typewriter for years, and that he and the barrow boy have concocted a false story—Guilty. But there is a third possibility and that is why I spent so much time on explaining to you the amount of proof required. The third possibility is that you are not sure about the typewriter, that you're not satisfied either way. In that case your verdict should be Not Guilty—the prosecution

will have failed to prove its case. Now, members of the jury,
you may think that the attitude of counsel for the prosecution
has undergone a change during this trial. Indeed, he admitted
as much. Well, members of the jury, the guilt or innocence
of a prisoner depends on the evidence, not on the attitude of
prosecuting counsel; nevertheless, you may well think, members
of the jury, that strange as are the coincidences which are
relied upon by the defence, they are not so absurdly strange
as to be incredible. I myself have only recently had an
experience which I would have said was as unlikely to happen
as anything could be. But it happened, members of the jury,
it happened. And what counsel for the defence very properly
asks you is—is it fair to reject the evidence of the accused, and
of the witness who was called about the typewriter, just because
of the unlikelihood of their story? Unlikely things do happen—
not every day fortunately—but they do happen from time to
time. Is it not better then to judge this case on the evidence
you heard, on the demeanour of the witnesses, rather than on
the probability or improbability of their story? Of course you
may take any probability or improbability into consideration,
but I suggest to you that, in doing so, you should not weight
the scales too heavily against the accused merely because at
first blush the chances of his story being true seemed small.'

After a few further words of guidance, the judge concluded
his summing up, and the jury retired to consider their verdict.
Meanwhile Miss Clinch, from becoming anxious as she noted
the *volte face* in the case of Brent, was becoming more and more
furious as she listened to the judge. Blithering old idiot, she
said to herself; this chap's guilty, ten times guilty, and he's
going to let him go. With difficulty she restrained herself from
trying to make a speech to the jury herself. Mr Waite tried to
console her while they were standing in the corridor.

'It's not your fault,' he said. 'We've just as much confidence
in you as ever. It's just bad luck. Anyway, he hasn't been
acquitted yet.'

'He will be,' said Miss Clinch.

And he was. Half an hour after they had retired, the jury returned to Court with a verdict of Not Guilty, and Mr Richmond was discharged. He went at once to thank his solicitor and counsel. Mr Tewkesbury was not there. He had been torn between missing opening time and hearing the verdict—and opening time had won. But after all he had heard the summing up and that was almost as good as an acquittal.

'I am most grateful to you,' said Mr Richmond to Stanmore. 'And now that it's all over I should like you to know one thing.'

'Yes?' said Stanmore.

'I'm right in thinking, aren't I, that if I now admitted my guilt to you I could do so with impunity? I couldn't be tried again as I've been acquitted?'

'That's perfectly true,' said Stanmore, 'but there is another reason too why you could tell me with impunity. I couldn't pass the information on. If the police could prove you'd committed perjury, you could be tried for that, but even if I wanted to give evidence on the subject I shouldn't be allowed to. So you can make a clean breast of it with absolute safety, Mr Richmond, if you think it would help your conscience.'

'Thank you,' said Mr Richmond. 'I wanted to be quite sure of that before I said anything to you, but now that I know I can speak freely, and that any admission of guilt could do me no possible harm, I want to tell you this.'

He paused to give emphasis to his words, which he repeated:

'I want to tell you this—that I am absolutely and completely innocent of the charge of which I was acquitted. I wanted you to have the satisfaction of knowing that you have defended an innocent man. But first I wanted to assure myself that you might not think I had an axe to grind. But, as you have told me, I have none. I could safely admit my guilt, if it existed, but it did not and I proclaim my innocence.'

'Well, I congratulate you, Mr Richmond,' said Stanmore. 'I confess I did not always think this would be the result.'

'It's an unfair world,' said Mr Richmond. 'Coincidences are

A few minutes later Mr Richmond left the Old Bailey by himself; Stanmore went to the robing-room, and Mr Tewkesbury went back to the private bar.

'The race is not to the swift,' he informed the barmaid, 'nor the battle to the strong.'

'There's no accounting for taste,' she said, 'but I like 'em swift and strong.'

'Well,' said Mr Tewkesbury, 'on consideration admittedly I like them strong.'

CHAPTER EIGHTEEN

Another Chance

NEWS of Mr Richmond's acquittal quickly percolated to the other prisoners awaiting trial—among them Arthur Green, a very old hand indeed, charged with obtaining money by false pretences.

'I'll tell you another coincidence,' he said to the warder who escorted him to the dock. 'It's my birthday.'

'Good hunting,' said the warder.

'Wrong way round,' said Mr Green. 'I'm the fox.'

'Put 'em on a false scent then.'

'I hope I have,' said Mr Green. 'D'you think this judge—oh—here we are. Sorry the journey's so short. I'll pay for my ticket when I leave.'

The warder winked. Mr Green went forward to the place he knew so well, facing the judge.

'Is anyone defending you, Green?' asked the judge.

'Oh—yes, my Lord.'

The judge looked at counsel's row enquiringly, but no one moved.

'Who is it, please?' he asked.

'Yours very sincerely,' said Mr Green.

'Don't be impertinent,' said the judge. 'You're defending yourself then?'

'If I may have that honour,' said Mr Green. 'To tell you the truth, my Lord . . .' he went on.

'Be quiet,' said the judge.

The jury were sworn, the charge read out and Mr Green pleaded Not Guilty.

Brent was again appearing for the prosecution, and he outlined the facts to the jury. To anyone who knew Mr Green's
previous career they had a familiar ring. Mr Green's business
was to buy goods on credit and sell them below cost price for
cash. As he either did not pay for them at all or only paid a
part of what he owed, he always made a substantial profit on
the transaction, until the creditors closed in on him. Then he
was duly prosecuted. He was usually convicted and sent to
prison for varying terms. When he came out he started all
over again. Brent, of course, said nothing of Mr Green's past
to the jury. He simply told them his most recent history, and
the precise charges in the case before them. Then he called his
first witness, who gave evidence that he had supplied gloves to
Mr Green to the value of thirty-five pounds, and that he had
not been paid for them.

'Did you believe the prisoner to be carrying on a genuine
business?' he was asked.

'I did.'

'Would you have supplied the goods if you had not so
believed?'

'I would not.'

'Thank you, Mr Taylor,' said Brent, and sat down.

'Well, Green, do you want to ask any questions?' said the
judge.

'If I may be so bold,' said Mr Green. Then, seeing the judge
frowning, he added: 'I never believe in using one word where
two will do, my Lord.'

'Start your cross-examination,' said the judge.

'Now, Mr Taylor,' began Mr Green, 'you've never met me,
have you?'

'No.'

'Until you saw me in the police court?'

'That's quite right.'

'How d'you know it's me?'

'What on earth do you mean?' said the judge.

'Mr Taylor says he's been cheated by a Mr Green. How

does he know that I'm the one. Common name, my Lord.
Common face, too, I'm afraid, my Lord.'

'He's never purported to identify you. He's simply produced
letters written to him which the prosecution say you wrote.
No doubt they will call another witness or witnesses to prove
that, if they can.'

'Thank you, my Lord,' said Mr Green. 'That is most helpful.
So, Mr Taylor, you have no complaint against me personally?'

'I don't know. If you had my goods, I have.'

'But you don't know that I had them?'

'If you wrote those letters you did.'

'But you don't know if I wrote the letters?'

'The police say you did.'

'Ah—we can't have what the soldier said, can we, my Lord?'

'No—that's quite right,' said the judge genially.

'So, apart from what the police say, you don't know that I
did write the letters or had the goods?'

'You wouldn't be where you are if you hadn't,' said the
witness.

Mr Green affected to look pained.

'Have you never heard of mistaken identity, Mr Taylor?'
he asked.

'Yes.'

'Have you never heard of an innocent person being accused?'

'I suppose so.'

'For all you know, I may be innocent?'

The witness said nothing.

'Don't be bashful,' said Mr Green. 'For all you know of
your own knowledge it may be someone else who did it, and
by some mistake—or coincidence——' Mr Green paused at
the word 'coincidence' and glanced at the judge—who told
him rather irritably to proceed with his question.

'—and by mistake or coincidence they hit on me. I have
been here before, you know.'

'I'm not supposed to say that,' said the witness.

'No, but I may,' said Mr Green. 'Give a dog a bad name

and hang him. This looks like Mr Green's handwriting, so we'll knock him off for it. That's the way it goes, isn't it?'

'It's nothing to do with me,' said the witness.

'Or me,' said Mr Green.

'Any more questions?' said the judge.

'The defendant rests,' said Mr Green, 'if you'll pardon the expression.'

'I will not,' said the judge. 'If you don't behave yourself I'll remand you in custody till next Sessions and we can start all over again then.'

'No more questions, my Lord,' said Mr Green.

The next witness gave his name as Robert Adams and gave evidence very similar to that of the previous witness, except that he had supplied tinned goods, not gloves. Mr Green rose to cross-examine.

'Your only complaint is that you haven't been paid, isn't it?'

'How d'you mean?'

'Well, if you'd been paid you'd have had no complaint, would you?'

'I'd have had my money.'

'Exactly. That's what's worrying you. Not having your money?'

'Of course it is. How would you like it? I've paid for the goods. I expect to be paid for them.'

'Absolutely,' said Mr Green. 'My sentiments entirely. May I say that I sympathize with you very much? I should have taken exactly——'

The judge interrupted. 'Now, Green, don't make speeches. Ask questions.'

'Merely introductory matter, my Lord,' said Mr Green, 'to help the witness understand.'

'If I think he doesn't understand the question, I'll intervene. Just you ask questions and skip the introductory matter.'

'Very well, my Lord. You'll forgive me, then, Mr Adams,' he added apologetically to the witness, 'if I don't make myself entirely plain in the first instance. Now, your complaint is that

the Southern & Eastern Counties Trading Company didn't
pay you?'

'That's one of my complaints.'

'Let's have them all,' said Mr Green cheerfully. 'You may
not get another chance. What are the rest?'

'That the Southern & Eastern Counties Trading Company
is just a high-sounding name for a swindler. It's a name to
trap people with.'

'The length of the name?' queried Mr Green.

'Everything about it.'

'You think it creates confidence?' asked Mr Green.

'I do.'

Mr Green smiled slightly.

'It shows the man you were dealing with knew what he was
about?'

'That he was a thorough paced swindler—yes, it shows that.'

'And a successful one?'

The witness smiled for the first time.

'Successful?' he asked. 'I've never been there,' he added,
pointing to the dock, 'but I shouldn't count myself very
successful if that's where I ended up.'

'My sentiments exactly,' said Mr Green. There was laughter
in the Court.

'Silence,' said the usher.

'Thank you,' said Mr Green, looking towards the usher.
'Now, Mr Adams,' he went on, 'what makes you think that
the Southern & Eastern Counties Trading Company is now in
the dock?'

The witness said nothing.

'Well?' said Mr Green. 'What makes you think it?'

'You are the Southern and all the rest of it.'

'Oh?' said Mr Green. 'And what makes you think that?
You've never seen the Southern & Eastern Counties Trading
Company, have you?'

'Well, of course not,' said the witness. 'You can't see a
company.'

'Can't you,' said Mr Green. 'It's not a limited company, you know.'

'Well, what is it?' asked the witness.

'You can't ask me questions,' said Mr Green, 'but I don't mind telling you. The Southern, etc., is just a name for someone. It might be you, for instance.'

'It is not,' said the witness indignantly.

'Only an example,' said Mr Green. 'Keep your hair on. I might have said it could be his Lordship.'

'If you think,' said the judge, 'that being alternatively pert, impertinent, impudent and irrelevant is going to help you either with the jury or me, you're very much mistaken.'

'Stopped one that time,' whispered Mr Green to one of his attendant warders. 'Forgive me, my Lord,' he said, 'it's not so easy to say the right thing from here. Now——' he paused for a moment and decided not to say that if his Lordship stepped into the dock and he stepped on to the Bench they would each learn some of the difficulties the other experienced. 'Now, Mr Adams,' he said instead, 'will you look at one of the letters you received?'

The witness was handed a letter.

'How's it headed?' asked Mr Green.

'The Southern & Eastern Counties Trading Company—proprietor F. Jones,' said the witness.

'Exactly,' said Mr Green. 'And can you see Mr Jones in Court?'

'Yes,' said the witness.

'Where?'

The witness pointed to the dock.

Mr Green turned to one of the warders. 'Your name Jones, by any chance?' he asked.

'Green,' warned the judge, 'I'm not going to have much more of this. You know quite well the witness meant you.'

'My name's Green, my Lord,' said Mr Green. 'It says so on the indictment.'

'You used Jones on this occasion,' put in the witness.

'You mean someone used Jones,' said Mr Green. 'Mr Jones, perhaps—which wouldn't be surprising.'

'You wrote this letter,' said the witness, 'and if you wrote this letter you're Jones—or you were then, anyway.'

'Did you see me write it?' said Mr Green.

'No.'

'Then how do you know I wrote it?'

'Because it's like other letters you wrote.'

'Did you see me write them?' asked Mr Green.

'No,' said the witness.

'Then, how d'you know I wrote them?'

'Because I do,' said the witness.

'Come now, Mr Adams,' said Mr Green, 'we're not in the nursery now. We're grown up. How do you know I've written any of the letters you've seen?'

'Because the police——'

Mr Green held up his hand to check him. 'We can't have that, you know,' he said, and smiled pleasantly at the judge.

'On consideration,' said the judge, 'I'm not sure that we can't, if you press the question. You're quite entitled to ask the witness how he knows something, but, if you do, why shouldn't he give the answer that someone told him?'

'I must be getting rusty, my Lord,' said Mr Green. 'I thought you couldn't. When this case is over, I'll go off to the library—the free library,' he added, with an accent on the 'free.'

'Well—never mind about that for the moment,' said the judge. 'It's right to say, isn't it?' he said to the witness, 'that you only know what you've said about the prisoner's letters because of what you've been told?'

'That applies to most things, my Lord,' said the witness.

'That may be right,' said the judge. 'You can only know things either because you've seen them happen or because someone has told you.'

'What about books, my Lord?' volunteered Mr Green, always ready to join in a legal or metaphysical discussion.'

'Books tell you things—not always correctly,' the judge added.

'What about stones, my Lord?' said Mr Green, 'sermons in stones——'

'That'll do,' said the judge, not quite as harshly as before. There was something about Mr Green that he could not help liking. If only he'd use his obvious talents to better purpose.

'Well, Mr Adams,' went on Mr Green cheerfully, well aware that he had made an impression on the judge, 'you agree, then, that, apart from what you've been told, you couldn't say any of the letters you had from the Southern & Eastern Counties Trading Company were from me?'

'I suppose I couldn't.'

'I'm very much obliged,' said Mr Green, and sat down. 'The defendant rests,' he whispered to one of the warders, and put his elbows on the front of the dock, and his head in his hands.

The next witness gave similar evidence, except that he had supplied ladies' underwear. Mr Green again established that the witness had never seen him personally before the prosecution and could not say of his own personal knowledge that Mr Green wrote any of the letters. The next three witnesses dealt respectively in soap, toffee and hardware, but otherwise their evidence was to the same effect. Finally, a detective-inspector was called, who said that he knew Mr Green by sight and was familiar with his handwriting. He identified all the letters written on behalf of the Southern & Eastern Counties Trading Company as written by Mr Green. With an air of greeting an old friend, Mr Green rose to cross-examine.

'We know each other well, don't we, inspector?' was his first question.

'Quite well,' said the inspector.

'You're in charge of this case, I take it?'

'I am.'

'When did you first come into it?'

'About four months ago. I can give you the exact date if you wish it.'

The inspector started to refer to his note-book.

'No matter,' said Mr Green. 'I just want to be sure that you were in it from the start.'

'Pretty well,' said the inspector.

'And didn't you say to yourself—when you were first called in—"this looks like old Arthur Green again?" '

'I'd rather not answer the question,' said the inspector, exhibiting that fairness which the police always show when they feel quite sure of a conviction.

'Very decent of you,' said Mr Green, 'but don't you worry about me—I want you to answer.'

'Very well,' said the inspector. 'I did.'

'You said to yourself—"this looks like old Arthur Green again?" '

'I did.'

'And you said it to other people too, I expect?'

'I did.'

'And then you came to see me?'

'Yes.'

'And you asked me if I'd been trading as the Southern & Eastern Counties Trading Co.?'

'I did.'

'And I said I hadn't?'

'You did.'

'And you didn't believe me?'

'I didn't.'

'And then you showed me some of the letters and asked if I'd written them?'

'I did.'

'And I said I hadn't?'

'You did.'

'And again you didn't believe me?'

'I didn't.'

'And then did you ask me to write something on a piece of paper?'

'I did.'

'With a view to showing the letters were in my handwriting?'

'Yes.'

'And I wrote whatever you asked?'

'You did.'

'And it didn't look the same as the letters, did it?'

'It did not.'

'And still you didn't believe me?'

'I did not.'

'Do you ever believe me?'

'It depends on what you say.'

'Then you showed me some letters—nothing to do with this case—and asked if I admitted writing them?'

'Yes.'

'And I admitted them?'

'You did.'

'Did you believe me that time?'

'I did.'

'Was that because I'd said what you wanted me to say?'

'It was because you were telling the truth.'

'So I do tell the truth sometimes?'

'I've said so.'

'Didn't you think it odd that when I wrote down what you asked me to write it didn't look the same as the Southern & Eastern Counties etc. letters?'

'No, I didn't.'

'Why was that?'

'Because I thought you were disguising your handwriting.'

'Trying to deceive you, inspector—an old friend?' said Mr Green deprecatingly. 'You wouldn't expect me to do a thing like that, would you?'

'Do you want me to answer that?' said the inspector.

'Perhaps not,' said Mr Green, 'if it embarrasses you.' Then he went on: 'You're not a handwriting expert yourself, inspector?'

'No.'

'Apart from these letters, there's nothing to connect me with the crime, is there?'

'I don't think so.'

'It wasn't my address where the Southern & Eastern Counties carried on their business?'

'I don't know—it was an accommodation address.'

'But it's owned by someone, I suppose. Someone lives there?'

'Yes.'

'And he couldn't identify me as the person who called for the letters?'

'He could not.'

'You had a good old try to see if he could, didn't you?'

'We put you up on an identification parade, yes.'

'With my full consent and co-operation?'

'Yes.'

'Indeed, I suggested it, didn't I?'

'I believe you did.'

'A dangerous thing to do, inspector, unless I was confident he couldn't identify me?'

'He was very short-sighted. Said he never saw you close enough.'

'Never saw *who*, inspector?' asked Mr Green sharply.

'I'm sorry,' said the inspector, 'never saw the man in question close enough to recognize him.'

'You're not suggesting that I chose him for that reason, inspector?' asked Mr Green.

'I wouldn't put it past you,' said the inspector, who had not been pleased at the man's refusal to identify Mr Green.

'Thank you,' said Mr Green, quite unperturbed. 'So that the position is that there is no evidence to connect me with the address of these swindlers, the Southern & Eastern Counties, there is no one who can say I am really Mr Jones, the proprietor; the only thing against me is the letters which you say are written by me, you're not a handwriting expert and the only time you got me to write it looked different. That's the case, isn't it?'

'That's comment rather than a question,' said the judge.

'I'd just like to know from the inspector that there isn't

anything else,' said Mr Green. 'I don't want them to leave out anything. After all, the taxpayer has to pay for all this. I want him to get value for his money.'

'Now, Green,' said the judge, 'don't overdo it. The real question in this case is whether you wrote the letters. The jury will be able to compare what is admittedly your own hand-writing and the letters themselves.'

'Of course, my Lord,' said Mr Green. 'And I'm not saying they don't look alike. They do. But coincidences do happen, my Lord. I'm not charged with writing badly, but with fraud.'

'Quite right,' said the judge.

'Lots of people write badly, my Lord, but they don't all stand in here because of it.'

'There wouldn't be room,' said the judge, 'and I should certainly be there if that were a crime.'

'That makes me feel more at home, my Lord,' said Mr Green.

'Have you any more questions to ask this witness?' said the judge.

'No, thank you, my Lord,' said Mr Green. 'I've finished him —with him, my Lord, I mean.' He sat down and a hand-writing expert went into the witness box to demonstrate by oral evidence and photographic enlargements that Mr Green had indeed written the incriminating letters.

'You seem very certain of yourself?' asked Mr Green, in his first question in cross-examination.

'I am certain.'

'You've made mistakes in your time, I suppose?'

'Everyone has.'

'Did you feel just as certain when you made those mistakes?'

'I can't say unless you refer me to the mistakes.'

'Then I shall have to trouble you,' said Mr Green, 'for some further details. What was your last mistake—in regard to handwriting I mean, of course?'

'I don't remember. It was a long time ago.'

'What was it?'

'I thought some figures were written by someone, but

apparently they weren't. Figures are much more difficult than words.'

'No doubt,' said Mr Green, 'but you have made a mistake in regard to words?'

'I have,' said the witness, 'but nothing like the mistake I'd be making if these letters weren't written by the same person. It's plain as a pike-staff. It doesn't need a handwriting expert to tell that.'

'Some people do write something like others?'

'Something like, yes, but not as near as this.'

'What would you say if I swore I did write the one lot and not the other?'

'What would I say?' repeated the witness.

'Yes.'

'I'd say you were a liar or had a very bad memory.'

'Suppose I had a twin brother—or a sister, if it comes to that. Don't they write alike?'

'Yes, but not exactly, not like these letters.'

'You came into this Court convinced it's me, didn't you?'

'I certainly did.'

'Doesn't give a chap much of a chance—if you're convinced before you come into Court.'

'He's not a member of the jury,' put in the judge, 'he's only a witness. It doesn't matter what he thinks. His evidence is what matters.'

'But his evidence is only what he thinks, my Lord,' said Mr Green.

'Yes—you're quite right,' said the judge. 'He's only giving evidence as to his opinion. It's a pity you didn't go to the Bar,' he added to Mr Green.

'D'you think it's too late, my Lord?'

'I think we'd better deal with this case first,' said the judge.

After the handwriting expert had finished, Brent closed his case and Mr Green went into the witness box. He stoutly denied that he had anything to do with the Southern &

Eastern Counties Trading Company. Yes, the letters did look alike, very much alike indeed—but it was a coincidence.

'Pity I didn't have them typed, my Lord,' he said in the middle of his evidence.

'Pity *who* didn't have them typed?' asked the judge.

Mr Green had seen his mistake.

'Pity the bloke in question didn't have them typed, my Lord.'

'I thought you said: "Pity *I* didn't have them typed," ' persisted the judge.

'It was a slip, my Lord,' said Mr Green.

'A very unfortunate one,' said the judge.

'I'm surprised I haven't made a lot more,' said Mr Green, recovering himself. 'Everyone says it was me, the inspector says he thought it was me before he'd investigated it, the hand-writing expert says it's me, all the witnesses say it's me; hang it, my Lord, I shall begin to think it *was* me, if it goes on much longer. If it had been a typewriter,' he went on, 'there'd have been no doubt about it, would there, my Lord?'

'Now, don't ask me questions,' said the judge.

'All depends where I'd got it from,' said Mr Green.

Eventually he finished his evidence and Brent addressed the jury for the prosecution.

'It is quite true,' he said, 'that very remarkable coincidences do happen, members of the jury, but can these . . .' and he held up the two sets of letters, 'can these be called coincidences? They are facts, members of the jury, and they speak a good deal louder than words,' and he looked at Mr Green sitting in the dock. Mr Green gave the jury an audible sigh. Brent sat down after a short speech and Mr Green made his address to the jury.

'Last time I was up for anything, I pleaded Guilty,' he said, 'and I got a very light sentence. Now, do you think that, as a man of some experience in these matters, I'd be foolish enough to tell this cock and bull story if it weren't true? Of course I wouldn't. I'd have pleaded Guilty and got another light sentence. 'Tisn't as if I didn't know what the prosecution had got against me. I got all that in the police court. Now, is it likely—I ask you as men and women of the world, is it likely? Of course it isn't. Why run your head against a brick wall? It doesn't make sense, does it? No, members of the jury, I pleaded Not Guilty because I was not guilty, and it wouldn't be right to convict me just because I have the misfortune to write like someone else. So let me off, will you please? I thank you.'

The judge's summing up was short. The jury took away the letters to examine them in their retiring room, but they were back in ten minutes with a verdict of Guilty. After his deplorable career had been read out in Court, the judge asked Mr Green if he had anything to say on the matter of sentence.

'My Lord,' he said, 'your Lordship and I have got to accept the verdict of the jury loyally, whatever we may think about it personally. To that extent your Lordship and I are in the same boat. Apart from that, we are in rather different positions. Now, what can I say on the question of sentence? It's rather difficult. I fully realize that the public have to be protected from people like the Southern & Eastern Counties Trading Company . . .' Mr Green said the last words with the kind of sneer which some prosecuting counsel might well have adopted. 'They ought to be sent to prison for a long time. As Arthur Green, I say that prison is the right place for Mr Jones. Mark you, my Lord, I'm not saying that Mr Jones hasn't brains and that if only he used them properly he might not have become a most worthy citizen—Southern & Eastern Counties Trading Company is a pretty good name really—it caught a good number of them—but your Lordship can't take that into consideration.'

'Indeed I can,' intervened the judge.

'I see,' said Mr Green. 'Well, as your Lordship will understand, my difficulty starts when Arthur Green is, for the purpose of argument, identified with Mr Jones. Without actually having known Mr Jones, it makes it very difficult for me to say anything in his favour. But I would urge that,

as far as is known, he, unlike me, has no previous convictions
and, as far as the evidence goes, he has always until now led
an entirely blameless life. What's sauce for the goose is sauce
for the gander, my Lord. And, just as I have loyally accepted
the jury's verdict that I have to play the part and accept the
sentence passed on Mr Jones—so your Lordship should accept
it and should ignore the past of Arthur Green who, for this
purpose, is Mr Jones, a first offender who—might I remind
your Lordship—might well respond to the treatment of the
probation officer. Moreover, if you send Mr Jones where he
may meet with hardened criminals you may convert him into
one. My Lord, I think that, in the circumstances, that is about
all I can say.'

Mr Justice Short hesitated for a moment or two before
passing sentence.

'Arthur Green,' he said eventually, 'you could probably
have made your name on the stage or as a writer, or in any
profession where a sense of humour is rewarded. Unfortunately,
you've chosen a criminal career where I hope a sense of
humour may help you after your sentence, as it cannot before.
Why you pleaded Not Guilty in this case, except for the purpose
of enjoying yourself at the public expense, I cannot imagine.'

'I'll tell your Lordship if you like,' put in Mr Green, so
swiftly that he could not be stopped.

'Well—why?' said the judge.

'I heard all about the last case, my Lord, so I decided to
have a go. Otherwise it was dead as a doornail.'

'You mean,' said the judge, 'that you hadn't prepared any
of that cross-examination or any of your speech to the jury?'

'Not a word, my Lord. But I'd heard that coincidences went
down well in this Court and, as that's all they'd got against
me, I thought I'd have a try. Sorry to have taken up your
time, my Lord.'

'Well,' said the judge, 'this only shows how incredibly
foolish you have been not to use your remarkable gifts for
some lawful purpose. I'm sorry you were misled by the rather

exceptional circumstances of the last case, but it oughtn't to have led you into committing perjury. I shall have to take that into consideration. I really don't know what to do with you. You don't even promise to go straight when you come out. You have a deplorable record and in the last thirty years you have been sentenced altogether to twenty-five years' imprisonment. However, you haven't been caught for a year since your last sentence, while you were caught ten months after your previous sentence. That's an improvement of two months, and I suppose I can say that it may have been due to your last sentence having been an exceptionally lenient one. I expect I'm wrong, but in the hope that you'll be able to make an honest living by writing your reminiscences for the newspapers when you come out, I'm going to sentence you to two years' imprisonment. It probably ought to be at least double that. But you won't get another chance, Green. I hope you'll take this one.'

'Thank you, my Lord,' said Mr Green. 'I'm always prepared to take a chance.'

CHAPTER NINETEEN

Holiday Plans

As soon as he had dealt with Mr Green, Mr Justice Short went home. Vivienne met him at the station. Meanwhile the police had released their only suspect as she was satisfied that the voice was different.

'Do you really feel none the worse?' the judge asked Vivienne on the way from the station.

'Fit as a flea,' she said, 'but all the better for seeing you.'

'Look,' he said, 'how would you like a sea voyage in the vacation—South America or somewhere?'

'Oh—darling, how lovely.'

'You'd really like it?'

'It would be heaven. Nothing to do except laze. It'd be good for you too. You are sweet to me. Thank you.'

She kissed him.

'You mustn't while I'm driving,' he said.

'You're not sorry you married me?' she asked, after a pause.

'What are you talking about?' he said.

'Well, I am rather a handful, I'm afraid.'

'I like handfuls.'

'And I have let you down from time to time.'

'That's all forgotten. I'll arrange for the tickets tomorrow.'

'You're too good to me,' she said, and kissed him again.

They reached home and were soon having a drink together.

'Darling,' she said, after their first drink, 'there is just one thing.'

'Yes?'

'You remember that last time you were really cross?'

'When d'you mean?'

'About the photograph you thought was me in the paper—
and I said it wasn't and you wouldn't believe me.'

'I tell you—it's all forgotten, and anyway I do believe you.
It was just a remarkable coincidence. There.'

He kissed her.

She said nothing for a moment. Then:

'Darling,' she said a little hesitantly.

'Yes?'

'I'm afraid it wasn't a remarkable coincidence. It *was*
me.'

He said nothing for a few seconds. Then he kissed her
again.

'Well—it's nice of you to tell me. Thank you,' he said. 'And
now it really is forgotten,' he added.

'I'd have hated to go away with you with that on my
conscience. I've wanted to tell you ever since I lied. I just
felt I had to lie then—in self-defence. I won't again, really I
won't.'

'I'm glad you've told me—but I tell you, it's all forgotten.
Now, where shall we go?'

The judge got down an atlas. They spent a very happy
half-hour considering their plans.

Not long afterwards a somewhat similar conversation took
place between Sally and Andrew Brent. He too got down an
atlas and they discussed where to go. Then Sally rang Vivienne
to chat about it to her, and finally they decided to go together.

'I'm so excited,' said Sally. 'I can almost smell the sea.'

'So am I,' said her husband. 'I'm going to try to give you
the best holiday you've ever had.'

'Darling,' she said.

'There's just one thing I want you to know before we go,'
said Brent.

'Yes?'

'I'm really finished with Polly Turner that was.'

She kissed him for answer.

'And it was never very serious anyway,' he added.

She kissed him again.

'I thought it'd be nice for you to know before we went.'

'I knew it wasn't serious,' she said, 'but it's nice to know it isn't at all.'

'And just one other thing,' he said. 'You remember when you wouldn't really believe about the coincidence of my running into her when we dined together last?'

'Well, I admit I found it pretty difficult, darling. But I do believe you now, darling, really I do. And anyway, it's all over—so what does it matter?'

'Well,' said Brent, rather uncomfortably, 'as a matter of fact you were quite justified in not believing me. It wasn't a coincidence. We'd arranged it on the phone.'

'I won't hear another word,' she said. 'I've never heard of Polly Turner or you dining with her or anything. All I know is that I'm going for a beautiful holiday with an adoring husband.'

'Adoring's right,' he said.

'So's adored,' she said.

Next morning Miss Clinch walked into a travel agency.

'I'm in a flipping rage,' she said to the rather surprised young man who attended to her. 'I want you to send me somewhere to cool off.'

The young man made various suggestions and eventually a date was fixed and a berth booked, and Miss Clinch left the travel agency feeling a little better.

Meanwhile Mr Richmond was making his arrangements. He too was going abroad. So he made a final call on Mr Tewkesbury and settled his costs. Before he delivered the bill, Mr Tewkesbury looked at it for a final check.

'My costs clerk drinks,' he informed Mr Richmond.

'Dear, dear,' said Mr Richmond.

'In consequence he leaves out some items and under-charges for others. You might have thought, sir, that he would be just as likely to overcharge or put in unjustifiable items. But not so. Drink does not have that effect on him. So there are no roundabouts to make up for the swings.'

'Why don't you get rid of him?' said Mr Richmond.

'Shortage of man-power, my dear sir. If I dismissed him I should have nobody.'

As Mr Tewkesbury was his own costs clerk this was strictly true.

'So, sir, if you have no objection, to avoid going into these petty little items which will take up your valuable time, I propose to add on a modest fifty pounds to avoid embarrassing you by charging too little.'

'What's the grand total?' asked Mr Richmond.

'The total,' said Mr Tewkesbury, 'though it can hardly be dignified by the word "grand" is—including disbursements— the exceptionally modest figure of nine hundred and ninety-five pounds eighteen shillings and threepence—say a thousand pounds. Then, if I add the fifty you so kindly suggested, that comes to one thousand and fifty pounds, sir—an awkward sum—say eleven hundred.'

'And cheap at the price,' said Mr Richmond. 'Make it guineas.'

'A troublesome calculation, sir, the conversion of guineas to pounds and shillings.'

'Very well, then,' said Mr Richmond, 'make it twelve hundred.'

'Guineas, sir?' queried Mr Tewkesbury, but Mr Richmond had gone as far as he intended.

'Too difficult,' he said, 'pounds.'

'I could get Miss Tompkins to help us,' suggested Mr Tewkesbury.

'What about your costs clerk?' said Mr Richmond, making out a cheque for twelve hundred pounds. 'He should be able to do it.'

'It's opening time, I'm afraid, sir, and my costs clerk is never available then. Which reminds me, sir, unless you have any

further business to transact I have a little business of my own
to do outside the office.'

Mr Richmond handed Mr Tewkesbury the cheque.

'Can I drop you anywhere?'

'That's most kind,' said Mr Tewkesbury, 'but I have my
own means of locomotion. Which reminds me, sir, the tank is
dangerously near the empty level. You will forgive me, sir?'
and after shaking hands with Mr Richmond, he was soon
hurrying round the corner to the nearest filling station.

Mr Richmond made one or two other calls, and then made
his final arrangements for sailing. Before doing so he sent a
dozen carnations to Miss Clinch.

'From a lame and bald admirer,' he put on the card.

Three days later he was sitting in a stateroom in s.s.
Doddington.

CHAPTER TWENTY

The Only Chance

SOME days after they had sailed, there was a knock on Mr Richmond's door.

'Come in,' he said.

A man put his head round the door.

'I've come to repair the telephone,' he said. Then he opened the door fully and came in—and both men laughed.

'Come in, come in, my dear boy,' said Mr Richmond. 'Everything's O.K. I've searched the passenger lists and looked carefully around. We don't want any more coincidences, do we? Where are the others?'

'They're all coming. We've kept to our cabins until you gave us the word.'

'Well done, well done,' said Mr Richmond. 'This calls for a celebration.'

He rang for the steward and ordered champagne.

'Now I want to know all about it,' he said, 'from the word go. You must have done your job superbly well. The change in the judge was remarkable.'

The man, who had been the first to visit Vivienne, smiled.

'It was quite fun really. She was a nice girl. I'm glad we didn't have to be too violent. I hate hurting women.'

'Well—you won't have to any more. We can safely retire.'

There was another knock at the door.

'If that's anyone to repair the telephone,' said Mr Richmond, 'tell him we're in.'

'I expect it'll be the three of them.'

Vivienne's first telephone man opened the door, and her second and both of Sally's came in.

'My dear boys,' said Mr Richmond, 'this is a great day. Do the honours, will you, George?'

The first man opened a bottle and very soon they were ready to raise their glasses.

'To our retirement,' said Mr Richmond.

They drank.

'Well earned, if I may say so,' he added. 'Oh—one thing,' he went on, addressing Vivienne's first telephone man. 'You didn't hit me quite hard enough. But fortunately you won't have to do it again. Poor Miss Clinch; she thinks you don't exist, that I pinched the money myself and knocked myself on the head. Poor girl. But she'll get over it. Now—tell me more. I don't want to miss any of it.'

'Tell us the net result first,' said one of the men.

'Of course, of course. I'm very sorry. Well—the expense was nothing . . . considering. I had to pay Ernest a thousand pounds, but he was well worth it. A barrow boy to the life. And a more reluctant witness I've never seen. My chap could hardly get a word out of him.'

'Is he quite safe?'

'Safe? Good gracious, yes. He's going back to the stage. No, don't look alarmed, I'm not serious. I've told him that he can join us one day if he wants to. But I was telling you the expenses. All told they didn't exceed five thousand pounds. That's everything. Both cases and your expenses too. Not bad on the whole. When I was a small boy I was very fond of playing—think of a number, double it. Well, that's what we've done, and we've only got to take five thousand pounds off it. But now I want to hear your side of the story. Don't leave out a word. I've just been telling George how brilliant you must all have been. The difference in that prosecuting johnny. If ever there was a case of before and after. He'd have eaten me alive before you fellows got to work on him, and so would the judge. But after you'd finished with them they nearly gave me something out of the poor box. Poor Miss Clinch. I sent her some flowers—she deserved some compensation. Carnations. Should have been a wreath really. Shouldn't be at all surprised if she jumped into the Serpentine or something. Just temper, you know. Nothing vicious. Now tell me everything. One at a time. George first.'

The four telephone men—two of whom had been the two Father Christmasses—told their stories in detail, interrupted every now and then by Mr Richmond, when he felt that they had left out some detail which he wanted to savour. When they had finished one of them asked him a question:

'What beats me,' he was asked, 'is how you managed to keep hold of the insurance money. Didn't they try to get it back from you until the case was over?'

'Indeed they did. But I told them quite truthfully that I had paid it away in four goes to a small limited company two of you may know by name—you should do, as you're the only directors and shareholders—didn't I tell you? Trust Joe Limited.'

'Yes—but surely they asked you questions about it when you were being cross-examined? Pretty difficult to lose a hundred thousand pounds on horses in that short time. Anyway, no one's going to put on twenty-five thousand pounds a time with a chap unless he's good for the money if he loses.'

'True enough,' said Richmond. 'Some awkward questions could have been asked about it—if I'd let them.'

'What d'you mean? You had to answer anything they asked you, didn't you, when you were in the witness box?'

'No, my boy, I did not. They say the law's an ass—well, it's a very friendly one. What I'd done with the insurance money was nothing to do with the charge against me, and the law doesn't allow them to ask me about it—not a question. Cross-examination as to credit it's called. Not normally allowed in the case of a prisoner. I can tell you, my counsel was wild about it.'

'How d'you mean? He wanted you to answer the questions?'

'I'll tell you. The only way in which I could be asked about the insurance money was if I gave evidence of my previous good character. Not being found out, by the way, is good character—very good character indeed. Well, of course, I'd told my counsel it was O.K. about the insurance money. Trust Joe Limited existed and had won the money from me. Its banking account could prove it. So far so good, but I wasn't particularly keen on having the identity and antecedents and assets of Trust Joe Limited being talked about in Court. You boys are quite right. A clever counsel—and they had one— might have tied me up in knots. But, of course, I didn't let on to my chappie about that. I was all cool, calm and collected about that—he need have no worries on that score, I said. Then, of course, he wanted me to give evidence of my not having been found out before—I beg your pardon, gentlemen, of my good character, and I had to think of a reason for not doing so. I think I did pretty well.'

'What did you say?'

'Well, first of all I said I was married, with a boy of fifteen.'

'You never told us,' said one of them.

'I usually tell the truth to you, you idiot. I'm more careful with other people. No, of course it was just a tale.'

'But what had it got to do with it?'

'I'm coming to that. I also said that when I was in the U.S.A. at the age of fifteen—which, of course, I wasn't—I was once convicted of pinching something out of a shop, and I said virtuously and grandly I wasn't going to have my son's ideals and reverence for his dad spoiled, as they would be if he learned of it. "I've led a blameless life since then and my boy thinks I can do no wrong. If you spoiled his illusions it might do him a lot of harm." "But, if you go to gaol, that'll spoil his illusions, won't it?" "Mr Stanmore," I said, "I am not going to gaol—repeat not." Well, the old judge put out a feeler or two to see why I wouldn't what they call "put my

character in issue," because he hadn't got anything against me
in front of him, but my counsel had to stand firm because I'd
told him he'd got to. He was wild with me, I can tell you—
and I expect old Brent was too. I expect he would have liked
to ask me about the insurance money, particularly as he was
appearing for the insurance company too. But he couldn't do
it. So here we all are.'

He opened another bottle and again they drank to their
future.

'It was a near thing, you know,' said Mr Richmond. 'How
on earth I came to use the same typewriter absolutely beats
me. It's so obvious. It's the only mistake I've made in twenty
years. It just goes to show none of us is infallible. But, by Jove,
it took a bit of getting out of. It was a pretty desperate plan,
but I couldn't think of any other. Fill them up with coincidences until they'd think nothing of mine. I can't thank you
boys enough. If you hadn't done it perfectly we'd all have been
sunk. Well—off we go again. Here's to us all.'

They raised their glasses and drank.

'Only one fly in the ointment, though,' Mr Richmond said
a little later.

'We've had England. And I shall miss her sometimes.'

'We could go back later on if we wanted to, surely?' said
George.

'Too risky,' said Mr Richmond. 'Just suppose you ran into
one of the girls. A coincidence, if you'll forgive me using the
word, if you like, but not by any means impossible—and just
not worth it. Once any of you were seen by the right girl
you'd be sunk, and if one of us sinks we all sink. Don't forget,
all four of you are identifiable—not by baldness or lameness or
typewriters or Father Christmas beards, but by your ruddy
great faces. Just think if one of those girls saw either of the two
of you who'd seen to her. In a bus, in a theatre, a train, anywhere you like. Things like that do happen. Why, I once sat
next to my form master when I was playing hookey. So was he,
fortunately. But those girls! They had plenty of time to look at

you, and they won't forget you in a hurry. No, it's unlikely but
it could happen. There've been no coincidences so far, and we
don't want any, do we? Even in South America it's not a
physical impossibility that one of them would run into you,
but that's the sort of coincidence that doesn't happen. That's
like our barrow boy and all the rest of them. The chances of
that happening are so remote as not to be worth considering.
Don't you agree?'

They all agreed.

'That's a risk we've got to take, and there's no real danger
of it happening. But how right the old judge was, and the
prosecuting fellow. Coincidences don't happen when you've
an axe to grind. They only happen when they're the last thing
in the world you want to happen.'

At that moment there was a crash, and they were all five
thrown to the ground. Then the alarm bell rang. Ten minutes
later the lights went out and the ship began to sink. There
had been a fog and their ship had collided with another. It was
night and the confusion was great, but somehow or other all
five men managed to climb into a boat and get away from the
ship before she sank. The other ship too was sinking. They
picked up people whenever they could, but the night was
pitch black and they could see nothing. Cries of distress were
their only guide. They picked up altogether three women and
two men. And then they waited, some of them cold and
shivering, but all of them thankful to be alive, for a rescue
ship to arrive. Luckily there had been time to send out an
S.O.S. and there was no loss of life. Not long before the dawn
they heard the fog signal of one of the rescue ships. They
could not reply, as they had no torch or dry matches. But the
fog signal got nearer and nearer, and it only required the light
of dawn to ensure their rescue. The sea was fortunately quite
calm. As the first light of dawn began they could see the
silhouettes of some of the rescue boats getting nearer and
nearer. Their safety was assured. All their heads were turned
intently in the one direction. But as it grew lighter and their

chances of survival grew to a certainty, the tension relaxed and they started to look at each other. For a moment Mr Richmond and his friends thought it was a nightmare. Sitting in the boat wet and cold, but very much alive, were—Mr Justice Short and his wife, Brent and his wife, and Miss Clinch.